Inhalt

Parker was dreaming again

Parker was dreaming again. Maybe he had been dreaming his whole life… His dreams had never been very satisfying and his life too had also never been satisfying. That is why his dreams were so disappointing. Or was his life disappointing because he had never had satisfying dreams? What comes first he wondered – dreams or reality.

His thoughts reminded him just now of the song "Dreams are my reality"

It was the 30th of December. Parker was awake in his dream and he was a wizard. If he had had more talent he thought he would write about muggles and wizards in the USA. There must be some there too. Parker was at the Abraham Lincoln school of Wizardry tucked away deep in the Blue Mountains in the Carolinas. There he was learning all the rules of Wizardry like Harry Potter in his time. Parker had been the middle child in a family of 7 Kids. His mother had always said there was something magic about him. And one day he woke up in his dream and found that the wizards had noticed his abilities and had taken him to that school. The school was named after Lincoln because he had also been a Wizard. But Lincoln had chosen to live among the muggles and help to save the country. The American wizards had found that too be very honourable and they founded a school for wizards and talented muggles in his name. At this school muggle with special talents learned along side of young wizards. The schools motto was integration of muggles and wizards because all wizards and muggles belonged to the same human family. But Parker was dreaming and he was having the usual difficulties that his dreams provided him. He guessed that there must always be an obstacle for him to grow but the troubles were nevertheless bothersome. Parker was having trouble following the number codes being taught in the class on Wizardry and modern media in the last hour of the day. The teacher Mr Count was an expert on the use of muggle inventions and the further development of these inventions for their integration in the wizard community. But the subject was very full magical mathematics and only the brightest wizards and muggles in the class could follow him.

But today one of the students, a brilliant girl of muggle birth with as much magical power as any wizard was presenting her research paper to the class. She asked Parker to present his wand but he could not find it. Hannelore, the girl, found the wand and gave it to Parker. He also knew where he had left his broom and his wizards staff that could make light like Gandalf the Wizard could in the Lord of the Rings.

After the class Parker and the girl were going to quidditch practice when suddenly Worm Wood appeared before them. He crawled out of the water and said that he knew Parkers secret code that he was supposed to learn in the Wizards and Modern Media class and he was going to capture Parker in his own cell phone using Parkers own number. Parker tried to summon help from Professor Schild, the head master of the school. But he failed to send his thoughts properly by telepathy, as he had been taught by Professor Schild.

Parker woke with a scream, soaked in sweat around his neck and was no longer in the dream. The dream was real but for the time being it was suspended. He knew he would return again soon to his Wizard. Professor Schild had told him this. That when real danger was at hand – and the dream was dangerous – he would be transported into his waking life if he called on Professor Schild in his mind. For now Parker was safe. But he would have to face that danger soon again and it would be necessary for him to finally face it and overcome it. Parker also knew that the dream reflected his feelings, that he could not function is his job and life as well as he wanted. He was fearful and frustrated and this was reflected in his wizard life also.

Parker and his fear. It's just a travesty

It seems funny but Parker knew that he had been living with his fear ever since he was 4 years old. He used to dream he was a planet in space that was threatened of being squashed in a collision of two larger planets – and he would wake up having this dream and still believe it to be happening to him. He would look for his parents and hope to find safety in their bed. He would dream that he was in danger of stepping on the wrong place and being in danger of triggering an explosion with one wrong step. His earliest dream found him in a car with his mother, driving down a narrow street with nothing but gray lifeless hedges on both sided of the street. They came to a house and drove up the driveway. Parker looked around the gray surroundings but when he looked back to where his mother was sitting she was gone. He had never been filled with as much fear again as the day he had that dream when he was barely 4 years old… And this letter he was looking at today reminded him of all this because he was making excuses for never returning to the United States to continue studying German…

Dear Dad

15Jan 1995

You may ask why I just don't pack the family and come back to the US. But, it is not so easy as it may seem. I never thought that before the force of routine and the establishment of house and home and family could lock one in to a certain area. But - it gets harder with every year to think about starting again from scratch. The 2 most important factors I see now are the health insurance and retirement income. The German health insurance system is so complete and comprehensive that there are practically no extra costs for hospital and medicine and I cannot imagine taking a family into the American freefall system again. For discussion's sake you can probably tell me a little about what you think. And then there is Hannelore's job. She earns very good money according to German standards. She also has what they call in America TENURE. Her job is permanent. Civil servants with tenure are called "BEAMTEN" in Germany and the State guarantees lifetime employment. If she came to America she would have to give up this great security.

He did not know how to get rid of this fear. But one thing he knew. It was time to pass this wall of fear so he no longer needed to sing the old song by KANSAS – Travesty The Wall

"It rises now before me, a dark and silent barrier between All I am and all that I would ever want to be… it's just a Travesty"

Parker and his Happiness and Debts

Parker read this letter from 1995 – It was from 17 years ago… Today he had forgotten what happiness was he had even found an stunning quote in Goethe's Iphigenie auf Tauris that seemed to match his feelings today

„Weh dem, der fern von Eltern und Geschwistern ein einsam Leben führt! Ihn läßt des schönsten Glückes nicht genießen"

Woe to him, who is far from his parents and siblings and therefore leads a lonely life, for he cannot enjoy even the most happiest moments of his life.

Parker thought if would be nice to go home again… but home was a place in the far past and it has dissolved like the mist of yesterday and his past had been carried away like the river's water of many springs gone by. Now all he had were his letters and a few family videos that depressed him just to look at…And his life was ruled by the money he had never had…

Dear Dad

18 march 1995

How is your business? How are your finances? Most of my finances run through Hannelore. I have my own bank account but it is 3000 Marks in the red. In Germany you can overdraw your account by a certain amount. It is like an instant loan but you have to pay high interest on it. You probably guessed, I never learned to handle money so that I would have an excess instead of a minus on my bank account. (Carl is into the wrapping paper in the corner of the office and making a mess - but he is happy). And my salary during the training is 726 Marks after taxes per month. 500 Marks go into the household and the rest I use to pay my student loans and odds and ends. I have no life insurance policies - I would like to get one if it were possible. Hannelore's bank account is 7000 Marks in the red each month at the end of the month. She earns 4500 Marks a month. Our house payments are 2000 Marks a month. And our groceries cost about 1600 a month - that is pure groceries and not car repairs and utilities included.

(I just changed Carl's diapers and gave him his cough medicine - he really puts up a struggle. You'd be proud of his strength!)

So , as you see above our finances don't make us happy. Our children make us happy but not our debts.

Parker the Dad

Parker had wanted to have seven kids – just like his dad. Today his three kids were grown and he was having trouble just taking care of two kids. He had not a penny to give them. He had given the financial care of them over to his wife from the moment they were born. He thought to himself, "If you had wanted seven kids why didn't you study for a profession in college. What were you doing there?" Parker had gone to college after high school and floundered around since day on of his college years. Yes he got a bachelors degree but it had been useless to him in getting a career and finding him his way in life. He never got a job upon which he would build his future and take over responsibility for himself – let alone feeding 7 kids – not to mention even 2. Yes his children were well taken care of! His wife had earned enough money to raise them – even though – it would have been better to be able to give them more money for their education. But they had been loved, fed and clothed and assisted along their way. No seven kids – his wife had needed a caesarian section for each of them. She was not the woman to have seven kids. This was perfectly okay with him. She just wasn't the woman for seven children – like he had thought of.

Now he was thinking about Carl… So often he had failed him. Carl went through several phases during a friendly father would have been a great boost to his personality. The phases were "The Lego phase", "The carpenter phase", "The outdoor man phase", "The musician Phase", and "The magic card phase". Parker had just plain failed him. Parker could not bring himself to be interested in spending time or effort in showing interest in these hobbies of his boy. It was pitiful and Parker had a very bad conscious. What had Parker been thinking? He had only wanted to spend his time "reading German" Whatever that was! He didn't read so much "German" Somehow he had never found the time. Carl had needed him to be his friend and Parker had just plain hadn't had the time. It reminded him of the "Cat's Cradle"

"The Cats in the cradle and the silver spoon, little boy blue and the man in the moon. When ya comin home dad? - I don't when. But we'll get together then son. Were gonna have a good time then!" Harry Chapin

Parker had never "Come home" for his son.

"18 Jan 1995

Life is moving along rapidly here. Sound familiar? Carl baby is now 11 months old. He is almost walking. Sometimes he surprises himself and lets go of the chair or table leg he is holding onto and just stands there freely for a few seconds. He grabs a wicker laundry, pulls himself up on his two feet and taxi-s across the room doing 100 mph baby speed. He has got the hottest feet of all the toddlers in the town. Carl still sleeps in our room. Baby is safest right under our wings. Daria slept with us for a year and a half. A good night's sleep of 7 or 8 hours straight is out of the question. He wakes up about every 3 to 4 hours and wants a bottle or tea or whatever. Sometimes I wake up just before he does - as if I am on his schedule now - which I am. Carl has 3 teeth below and 4 teeth above. His favorite food is spaghetti and beef out of a baby glass. When he takes a sip of orange juice out of glass he makes a real sour face - but asks for more punishment just the same. Hannelore says he is just like me that way. He likes it best when his sisters are around and there is lots of noise. When music plays in the radio Carl dances up a storm. We took him with us to see a song and dance routine of the local theater club and began clapping before the first number was over. The people around us were watching him instead of the actors on stage. Every time he sees one of us he smiles instantly-having two older sisters that spoil him he has become a real charmer. Hannelore says he is a typical American baby because he loves to go in the car. He is just loads of fun!"

Tuesday – 12 Sept 1995

"Carl is sleeping at the moment and I can write a few words in peace. When he is awake and around the computer he always wants to fiddle with the keyboard and it is impossible to get anything done. He fell asleep around 11:00 A.M. on our way home from clothes shopping. I went out with him this morning and bought him 3 pairs of overalls and two nice shirts. Every shirt goes with all the overalls so he will be well equipped with clothes now. Every day I had to really scrounge for what to put on him so I decided to stock up his supply today. Carl had a ball at the store. One sales lady was helping me and the other was chasing him around the store. Carl was giggling and laughing. In intervals we would round him up and try a few pants and shirts on him to see if they fit. He was well behaved and pleasant while we dressed him up and out like a little doll. The sales clerks were charmed with his pleasant nature and smiles."

Parker, religion and nursing

Parker dreamed about nursing again last night. The dreams kept coming back to him. It was like he was being forced to nurse again - he did not know why. But it felt like a forced punishment. When he dreamed about nursing he was always aware that it was a dream but he did not wake up but instead doggedly made his way through the dream. He knew the dreams were about fear and responsibility. He seldom ever made it to actually performing any nursing tasks in his dream. Mostly it was about getting to the right place on time or not or about whom was going to do what tasks during the shift he was supposed to work. Most of the time he did not even get started with the shift but floundered around trying to find out who was sick and what they had and in what rooms they were laying. Last night Parker actually got into a patients room and had his hands on tubes and drainage bags. The patients was a young man – but Parker could not figure the young mans sickness and Parker felt a vague dread while all the while the patient was trying to get out of bed and was twisting and pulling and stretching on his various attached tubes and bags. It was the morning after the dream when Parker came across this letter. Parker's Mom had been a nurse too but she had never mentioned that she had felt anything like dread or fear of nursing. Parker's Mom had been a guiding light in inspirational matters. Though this inspiration had never helped Parker really find a way for himself it had somehow inspired him to search for truth in his own life. Parker had always found "Uncertainty". But "Uncertainty" had become a marker of "Truth" for Parker. If anyone had claimed to know the one true way to God that person was certainly mistaken. The search for God was an individual path for each person and the comprehension of truth is only as wide as the field of vision of each person's awareness. God and truth were larger than us all and that was certain.

11 April 1995

"I hope you had a wonderful time at your retreat - nice friendly people, good weather and a lot of enlightening personal insights!

I was surprised to hear that you think your life is stagnant because you have been very busy - coming and going. What kind of change or experiences are you hoping for? Just keep writing me more letters and you can be sure that you are doing something valuable and that you making someone happy!!!!

You asked me how my work in the urology surgery was... I had a fun time and the operations that I helped on were fascinating! It was amazing to look into a live body and watch what the doctors were doing - cutting, sewing and poking around with their gloved fingers in peoples kidneys and urin bladers and abdominal areas. Now I am back on a regular surgical recovery ward. The people are nice there so work is not too bad at the minute.

Thank you for telling me to slow down and enjoy the moments of life as they come. I am really trying to do that these days. I am listening to my positive mental attitude tapes daily again. It helps my mood.

That is all for now - Love Parker!"

Parker had forgotten who he was

Parker had com to Europe only half baked. First of all it was ridiculous to have come without any money and without a job. He had not realized how helpless he could get. He was the true "prodigal son". He had taken his love, energy and his vulnerability – these had been his inheritance – his true gifts from his parents – his portion of his father's and mother's wealth. And he had squandered it away – He had never used these talents in his world. And he did not have the grace of the prodigal son who had returned to his father just in time to reunite and gain his true inheritance which was the presence and love of his parents and his family in his own life. Parker had forgotten his own value and had never found fertile soil for his soul to grow on in the world he had ventured into. The grass had not been greener on the other side. And now 30 years down the road he had truly forgotten who he was. He wanted to remember now …

Parker's own daughter had been trying to wake him up out of his stupor. But it was like being lost in fog or being wandering in a dark forest.. The letters Parker had written were like the crumbs of bread from the fairy tale Hansel and Gretel. And his daughter was like Gretel – who instilled hope and motivation to find the way back…

"18 March 1995

Ah... it feels good to talk with you again. I really enjoy putting my thoughts to paper - even if they are simple and not earth shattering in their content. What ever came out of your writing or typing course? In August 93 you typed me a letter. Are you still interested in writing or typing? By the way, your written words (from the letters you have sent me over the past 2 or 3 years) are beautiful and like a little inspiration treasure chest for me. I was just looking through some of them and they are full of loving inspiring thoughts. For instance:

Oct 15 1993

.... Parker, your letters are very wonderful and you're changing and growing is very evident...

August 18, 1993

... The past is gone and we need to leave it behind and look for new opportunities... of course you can succeed if you choose to and start telling yourself that you are capable.

... Enjoy your time at home and savor it. Don't let anything diminish your pleasure in it... it is important to do well at anything we try. We do not have to try to be loved or respected if we are giving it our best shot.... don't judge your thoughts. Thoughts are just that and are not to be judged, but to be retained or dismissed..."

Parker and Money Madness

Parker had never had much money. It had been barely enough when he was living by himself. But when his shortage awareness had been combined with his wife's awareness of shortage it had become too much and the two were always short of money. Parker's wife surely earned enough! In fact she earned more that than many people in Germany and her income would have been managed by many with the result that there was plenty to go around. But Parker's wife always "felt" she did not have enough money and Parker had always "known" he had not had enough money and these tow attitudes combined had created the perfect "scarcity syndrome". It was a perfect match. It had worked well and they had gotten along just fine but they carried this mystique of "no money" with them wherever they went.

Parker used to add up in his mind how much he owed his wife – because he earned less than her. He figured he owed her 24 thousand dollars for each year they lived together. But he had never earned this much and after 20 years he stopped counting because he couldn't think of that much money in one pile.

For years he had tried to manage the budget for the family and had produced the result of going farther into debt each year. Finally he admitted that he could no longer do it alone. Then his wife had summoned her courage and took back her own bank account – which she had not looked at in years. She had to borrow money to get out of the insolvency – and was extremely angry at Parker for not telling her earlier of the situation. Of course he was certain he had told her several times … Now she was managing the situation… but the feeling of scarcity still ruled … they got by but there were no vacations and other perks always the feeling of just getting by…

"10 June 1994

Nancy, thank you for the new pharmacology book and the newspaper! The book is very interesting and I am happy to read about what is happening in Michigan/Detroit. Hannelore loves to read comics too! She and I miss sitting at the breakfast table on Sunday and reading the Sunday edition of some U.S. paper with comics and journal section and rolls or bagels.

I am not getting very far with this letter. Today is Eileen's birthday. I have enclosed a birthday card for her with money as a present because I had no idea what she might want for a present.

Life goes on as usual here in Germany. Nothing much new is happening. Thw weather is rainy. Our building project is moving at a snail's pace. (even slower) Mom and dad are supposed to sleep in the new bedroom that we are building over the garage and utility room. But I am not at all sure that it will be done by the time they get here. Our bricklayer/carpenter did not come all this week again!! Hannelore is really mad at him. She was mad at me too yesterday because I spent the rest of the grocery and house money planned for the week yesterday - on things we needed - but she wanted to stretch it out for the rest of the week- She had to go back and pick up another 200 Marks. We went way over our budget of 400 Marks per week for the past few weeks. The money seems to be getting shorter all the time. It does not buy nearly as much as it used to.

So that will be all for now. Once again - thank you for the book! I will send some postal money to you in a few weeks.

Give my love to everyone you talk to in the family.
Love Parker"

Parker was the most crippled man he knew

Parker was the most crippled man he knew. He did not know how to heal himself. He did not believe he could do it. He wanted to write a book and have it published and make money that way… He had felt this way for 20 years. He knew his problem and had reached the bottom of it years ago but moving out of that place seemed impossible. It was like trying to scale a wall that was too steep and too tall … it seemed hopeless…

"Dear Dad,   15 January 1995

This is my first letter in 1995. Enclosed is a payment for my loans. It is a little late so could you please put it in the mail as soon as possible? I have had the money in the desk drawer for 3 or 4 weeks but I just didn't get around to sitting down and printing the envelopes for the Sate of Michigan. and writing a letter to you to go with the money.

It was really nice talking to you at Christmas!!! Time really flies because here it is already towards the end of January.

I have had a rough time over the past 3 months! I am starting to feel better now. It is a shame that I couldn't always remain positive. I hope I did not worry you all too much.

I had been going through a process of coming to terms with myself. I don't like living so far away. As long as I was in Bremerhaven and saw Little America every day I didn't feel so bad or so isolated. But now where there is nothing left in my life from America and I am actually working in the German system. I get homesick for American things a lot more.

You may ask why I just don't pack the family and come back to the US. But, it is not so easy as it may seem. I never thought that before the force of routine and the establishment of house and home and family could lock one in to a certain area. But - it gets harder with every year to think about starting again from scratch. The 2 most important factors I see now are the health insurance and retirement income. The German health insurance system is so complete and comprehensive that there are practically no extra costs for hospital and medicine and I cannot imagine taking a family into the American freefall system again. For discussion's sake you can probably tell me a little about what you think. And then there is Hannelore's job. She earns very good money according to German standards. She also has what they call in America TENURE. Her job is permanent. Civil servants with tenure are called "BEAMTEN" in Germany and the State guarantees lifetime employment. If she came to America she would have to give up this great security.

It is sad for me now that I live so far away. I almost call it a mistake of my youth. The ideal situation would be to overcome this "mistake" or distance barrier by making a lot of money and becoming independent. I have sort of capitulated to the fact that I will not ever make alot of money. The pay as nurse in Germany will bring me less than half of what Hannelore earns in her job. She earns about 4500 D-Marks take-home pay a month after taxes. I will earn about 1900 D-Marks when I am done with my training. The nice thing about working in Germany however is that I already get 5 weeks and 4 days vacation a year in Germany! Besides that fact that what I really wanted to do wa to study Psychology and German after I finished in Bremerhaven. Of course you don't earn any money when you study in Germany and the degree takes 5 years! So I decided to take the short road to a career and Hannelore was willing to put up with the small amount of money I would earn during the training and she was totally against me studying. I wasn't sure I could succeed on the German University either so that is why I started the nurse's training. A bird in hand is worth 2 in the bush.

So I have still got some work to do to get back into harmony with myself. You might say I should practice affirmations. But believe it or not I have never been much of a prayer-man or affirmations type.

When compared to others I know that I have a very great life. I will list some of my blessings here: A beautiful wife, wonderful health, and wonderful children, wonderful and loving parents, all my brothers and sisters and their support, a beautiful home and community to live in, plenty to eat and safe steady income for me and my wife, just all around super living conditions. So, I feel real good when I list all that!!!"

Fear not the white page

Parker loved the white page. What he didn't love was discipline. He wanted to play. His favorite activities when he was young was playing football in the yard with the other kids and his other favorite activity was sitting under a blanket on the register where the warm air for heating the room came out. Here he would lie or sit in the late evening or early morning hours when the living room was empty listening to music cassettes and just dreaming away his time. But what did this have to do with the white page? Even before he could write or read he was scribbling lines on white paper, imitating what he thought was cursive writing. And from the age of 14 years old he began keeping a journal and began to write letters to friendly cousins that came from other parts of the country to visit him. Some of these letters he got back from his pen pals and liked to take them out every once in a while and read them.

But the discipline it would take to write a story or even a song had always eluded him – or better said - he could not make himself sit still long enough and think twice or even once about the thoughts that were always coming to him. He had thought of a thousand beginnings to a story but after the first few lines nothing new occurred to Parker of how the story could go further.

He hated the work of figuring anything out. How would he turn his own self into a story? What would happen to his creations like "Snail Father" or "Foot"? How would Joseph discover the darkest secrets of the Vatican in its Jesus Conspiracy? How could a success story about himself which he had had not experienced ever come to pass? He hated puzzles. He hated crossword puzzles. He hated playing games and though he loved languages he hate the exercises of figuring out and writing out the verb forms in all variations. It simply was not his thing. He never became an inventor. Most of all he loved to copy things down. Or as a child he had once written out the numbers from 0 to at least 10,000 on several pages of paper. Parker's wife says, "Parker loves to read telephone books." Even his job consisted of doing the same thing over and over and over and over again, "Hello my name is Parker. How can I help you? Yes the amount on your account is so and so."

And while doing these mundane repeating his mind was free to wander, without discipline, without a direction and without a demand on his attention to anywhere he may find himself. His dreams were also of the same chaotic nature. It was hard for him ever to write down a dream because people, and places and objects changed without difficulty in the middle of a thought – he might be flying, running of driving a car all within a few seconds just getting from one side of the room to the other. And even worse his dreams were short and never ended almost before they began. Just like his stories – all of his dreams ended after the first scene. And almost all of his dreams were forgotten if he awoke even before he was able to walk from his bedside to the door of the bed room. A few dreams he had noted down, but his attempts at recreating what he had dreamed where like the attempts of a child trying to paint his first "Kopf-füßler" (German for "Head-feeters) They consist of just scratched circles and lines when trying to draw a picture of "mom and dad"

He was able to close his eyes and while still awake hear and see images very clearly in complete detail but to try to put them down on paper was futile attempt for him. However he could not force these images – and they dissolved from his inner screen just as involuntarily as they came.

So he did not fear the white page – he feared the discipline of filling it with anything else but numbers, circles and lines.

Parker and Thanksgiving

Missing the holidays had been a real problem for Parker. There was no Thanksgiving, there was no 4th of July, there was no Labor day and no

Memorial day – not to speak of the days of the Presidents! Identity is holiday. So Parker had shed these days like a skin and these days and many other events had long been forgotten. What was left for him? It was all in the name of learning German and came the in path of his flight from Julie. There is a new song in the radio - (he heard it after 30 years of missing Julie) – it is a song that appears to fill the idea of his thoughts right now. It went „*I wish I had missed the first time that we kissed.* “ If Parker had not been there to meet her he would not have been here to hear this song and would never have missed those holidays and if he had been lucky he may have never missed himself – like a bus that left 2 minutes early. It was also like a bus that never came and left him standing there freezing on a cold an icy evening. He wondered who he had missed on those busses – and thanked God for the cold feet he had gotten.

Cold feet would have served him well 29 years ago to keep him from getting on that plane that took him away from all those holidays.

Now there were no holidays and no family and no father to write to. His dad had died on one of those famous holidays – on the 25 of December 2001 – and Parker had missed that too. But in his mind Dad was still there….

„Dear Dad,   28 November 1994

I want to thank you for calling us this week. Sorry I missed your call but Daria and Gesa were happy to talk to you!

I did not send you a Thanksgiving Day card but I hope you had a wonderful turkey day with joy, good food, family togetherness and relaxation. This holiday is not celebrated in Germany and both Hannelore and I had to work. We did not have turkey either. Turkey's are expensive here. But I've decided to buy one for certain next year (they cost 40 Marks DM for a 6 lb turkey) and take a day of vacation. I really missed having the holiday. Hannelore and I both feel like moving to the US if it were possible. But I am taking this nurse's training and she is a well paid teacher - which she couldn't be in the US to start out with. Besides we just renovated the house and we have to stay here a few more years. We would love to take a vacation to the US in 95 but our house and car payments and living costs are so high that we go into the financial hole every month.

On the day you called us I had been thinking about you very intensively. I wonder if you have picked up on my thoughts.

As you know I am working again. As a matter of fact I am working 13 days straight including 2 weekends back to back. Work isn't much fun at the present. I don't know why. I really do not like the ward where I am working. The nurses and male nurses are all a bit older and set in there ways. I was happy that I did not have to work there for 5 weeks. I wish I could apply the principles of Jack Boland and really begin to love it. But even after all the tapes I have listened to and all these years - I still find it impossible to follow Jack's advice in daily life.

Another thing I realized is that with a wife and family I should be concerned with making money and building a financial base in order to support my family and secure their financial future. Foremost responsibility for a father should be to support his family and set up their future financially. I have been concerned with myself and having time to read literature and learn languages. But there is no immediate money to be made just learning a language and reading to read.

So... everybody is doing fine here. Carl is getting big and he is ruling the household already with his little commanding voice. Gesa and Daria have their regular school routines everyday. Gesa has been very busy after school because she is putting on a play with her drama class at school. They practice 2 to 3 hours almost every day. The performances just started last week. The audience loves them. Hannelore is a hardworking 4th grade teacher. I am working everyday like I said. Thank you guy for all the packages you sent in the mail. Your Thanksgiving card is beautiful.

That is all for now. Please send another check to the State of Michigan. 50$ is enclosed. Could you write a check and drop it in the envelope and mail the letter on its way? Thank you. I love you all very much. That is all folks ... „

Parker and the Truth

In reality Parker had never been honest with himself. He could never have been a nurse! He was much too self-centered and much too scared of sickness to walk in the valley of death. For him it was too close to the other side. He could ignore his fear of death almost exclusively because he was so healthy and strong. This changed when he began his training to become a nurse and then he got his appendix out. He no longer felt complete. Now not only his spirit was cracked but his body was no longer invulnerable. He was scared shitless – and this was symbolized in his appendicitis.

„Dear Dad,   17 November 1994

It is that time of the month again. I have enclosed an envelope with letter and 50 dollars for the State of Michigan. Please write a check as usual and send it along to the State.

Perhaps I could just write you a little note to let you know how I am doing?

It has been a rough month. When I got the pains in my lower right hand belly I couldn't believe what was happening - I looked in my anatomy book and then realized it was my appendix. I was afraid of being operated on! But by the time I was operated on I was past the fear - I just wanted to get relieved of the pain.

And the recovery was hard. They kept telling I had high blood pressure while I was in the hospital and the wound got infected and it hurt to get out of bed and I was worried that there was more wrong with me than just my appendix. I have been in a very bad mood for the last month. I know it is anti Master Mind and negativity but I just couldn't help it. I don't know myself anymore. I have become a real worry type of person.

Right now I am in a really bad mood too.

Do you have any suggestions at this time how I could get over this and get on with life?

Now I give you some positive news. Carl is really getting big and strong now. He is crawling all over the house and he can pull himself up on his two feet and stand up holding himself up with just one hand. I have had lots of time to watch him since I have been at home for the last 4 weeks. It has really been a joy to watch his progress. He is even starting to talk now. He says MAMA upon command and he rattles a lot of things like DAD-a DAD-a. He likes to throw his toys out of his play pen and down from his high chair. He likes to make loud noises with spoons. He claps his hands like patty cakes and he is interested in everything. Daria is just the greatest big sister to him. She loves to play with him and make him laugh. She carries him all around the house even though he is more than half as big as her. Carl squeaks with laugher and joy simply at the mere sight of Daria. Those two are simply good friends. Trying to change his diaper is like trying to hold a jumping bean still. He wants to turn over on his belly and hop right off the changing table. He is strong. He hates to have his nose wiped or get skin cream rubbed on his cheeks. When the doctors want to look in his ears or throat they are just amazed at how strong he is.

Well, I hope you feel good. Your welfare is my concern. Too bad you are so far away. That's all for now. „

Parker - „It's My Job".

Years later Parker was reading this letter „*It's My Job*". He had blamed his wife for his situation. But he could also thank her for his situation. He blamed her for his failure in his career – he had never had one. He thanked her for the family she had given him, his children. He said to himself, "No one, but she, had ever given me"*anything more beautiful in my life"* The dumb thing was he had felt so sorry for himself that he had forgotten how to appreciate his children. Parker had left his father and mother behind 28 years ago. He had mourned the absence of his parents in his adult life. They were the ones who would have given him the absolute support he had so longed to find in his wife. But she had said from the beginning, "Parker, solve your own problems! She had only turned her shoulder in distain when he showed his fears and weaknesses. She was a fearful one herself. He had assumed "his woman" would have the quality of helping him bear his deepest fears and sorrows. She had failed to attend to him in this way and to the contrary she had longed herself for a husband with courage and strength and assertiveness. Parker's wife had expected him to not be "co-dependant". It was in his saddest hours that he wished that he could have felt the presence of his parents once more. Who was there in Germany to fill this void? Parker had kept his emotions to himself as a teenager but had believed that if only he could find a woman to love him that he could pour out his feelings and his woman would love his wounds away. He would then have the heart and strength of a lion. It was like he was the tin man, the scarecrow and the lion all in one before they met the Wizard of Oz. His woman would "give" him everything he needed for happiness, joy and success. It occurred to him… this is why he had never relied on "God". These traits were to be forthcoming from his faith in his woman. And the first real woman he had expected to fill the bill had been Julie. She had quickly rejected her role as his Wizard of Oz. And when his wife did not fill this bill but at the same time didn't play her expected part in his drama his thoughts turned to Julie. In his heart he had never accepted her "NO". But she had said no. To turn his thoughts to her was just like watching the movie about Dorothy over and over again and never learning the moral of the story. And so, the "Wizardess of Oz" lived on in his heart. And that is why he had sought her in Germany. Unfortunately it had become obvious in a matter of days within his arrival to Germany he had not landed in the Emerald City. He would not be trimmed and polished and taken to the Wizard and get the "stuff" he needed. In fact even the Real Wizard of Oz had said. You already have what you need within you to fill up your void. And his journey through Oz had lasted much longer than Dorothy's. And his journey had never taken him back to his parent's home. Because unlike a movie that can be replayed over and over again life has no rerun button and time passes and people pass and change and once you leave Kansas you can never go back again. So it becomes your job to stand up in life and be your own wizard. And if you live near your own parents you can go back from time to time and rely on them to strengthen your resolve... But Parker realized now „*It's My Job*". *And that's alright by me - like Jimmy Buffet sings* and this letter reminded him of how close he was to home all the time and never knew it. It felt good to Parker to write this ...

17 March 1994

"Outside the world looks wintry with the melting snow but the sun is shining very brightly and the birds are chirping in anticipation of spring. We have our first spring flowers in the garden. They are called easter bells and look like miniature tulips. In the woods the whitethorn tree buds have turned green and forest floor is just starting to get green. On elder tree the first green leaves have sprouted. Spring comes earlier here than in Michigan.

By the way, Carl, our baby is sleeping in our bed right now and he looks so sweet. There is nothing like a precious little baby. He smells so good and his skin is so soft. Today he smiled for the first time. He is growing fast and he has grown out of all his first baby clothes already. He has gained 2 pounds and grown almost 2 inches already. When I look at him I think I have never seen anything more beautiful in my life. I know that I thought the same thing about Daria too but I had forgotten the overwhelming impression of the feeling. Carl has gotten smart and is nursing well now and sleeping good. He likes to be held while he is falling asleep and sucks ambitiously on his pacifier - spitting it out from time to time and crying until we stick it back in his mouth.

I am constantly listening to the Jimmy Buffet tapes you sent me. If you have any more feel free to send them. I listen to them on my 30 minute drive to work.

One of my favorite songs is the song „It's My Job". And thanks for the newspaper!!! I enjoy reading a local newspaper from time to time. I hardly see anything American anymore."

Parker and the Dead Sea Scrolls or German

Parker had failed himself, because he had never taken the responsibility for how things were inside him. He had known right from the start what was right and what was wrong for him. But instead he kept on down the path he had taken in the pursuit of is life with her. She had occupied his mind ever since he met her. She had occupied his mind long before he had met her. But he had expected his journey with her to bring him happiness. It had not. Happiness had been experienced in the moments when he had been immersed in the joy of learning. He had loved the moments reading about the alternative Gospels of the Dead Sea and of the truths of the early Christianity that had been hidden by the Catholic Church and by the Governments that cooperated with the established organization that called itself Christianity. He had been happy when he had been learning German and hearing about the progression of ideas as presented in German Literature. Instead he had believed in the motto…"first the woman and then happiness". It has turned out for him "first the woman and forget the happiness". Everything had gone wrong and even from the start. He had never had the courage to stop himself on this path of regret and sorrow… and he did not know why… But in this letter he had found it is clear that he should have stopped on this path even from the day he began. Parker said to himself – You took on the responsibility of being a father and you dare not ever fail in this duty. He had had wonderful children but had suffered horrible depression because he had not followed his conscious. He had been a good father but he never had been a great father. He could have been a great father if he had taken the responsibility for himself right from the beginning. Instead he had blamed everyone else and was still doing it. So he decided during his vacation the last few weeks to stop complaining and moaning and mourning for what he had not done and to begin accepting life as he had made it for himself… He would now live… from this day forward and no longer in the past…

"10 August 1996

It is way past due to write again. I have been too busy worrying about my exam to sit down for 30 minutes and write you a letter. Well it is Saturday and everyone is off to school. School is in session again in Lower Saxony and it is the tradition that the new first graders have their orientation and first day of school on the first Saturday after school is in session. Hannelore has a second grade class but all the kids have to go to school to greet the new kids. Gesa went with her and Daria went to her own school, she is in the 4th grade this year.

I was worried that my practical exam wouldn't be so good. But I was surprised because it turned out even worse. It was very bad. The grade, good, bad or failing is not revealed until all parts of the exam have been taken on 20 September 96.

And, as you may know Hannelore is very disappointed. She says I will never accomplish anything. She says she is done with worrying about my job future -(which is good because it is my problem anyway!) and is angry that I am not earning my share of the family income. She thinks I am too easy on myself and give up when things get rough. That makes her angry because she is always very hard on herself in these matters while I refuse to punish myself.

Of course you know what I really wanted to do was study German again. That was 4 years ago - but I was afraid I wouldn't be successful and Hannelore would have gone on the warpath if I had done that. So I have spent theses 4 years wishing I would have done the other thing and although nursing has been interesting I haven't really had my heart in the matter. What is worse is that I have been worrying about getting every sickness that we studied for the past three years. Work on a ward is not bad but I did not really get along with any of the people I worked with. A large portion of the nurses smoke and they smoke in the break room so that every break I was confronted with the terrible nasty cloud of smoke. I smell like smoke when I com home and my nursing outfits all smell like smoke when I go into the patient's rooms. Most of the time I am unsure of myself and react accordingly. The week before my exam I worked intensively with a registered nurse - who smokes and who I don't like - and he just shook his head and said I wasn't in any way, shape or form to be a registered nurse. He said I was unorganized and refused to take responsibility for my patients. This was the atmosphere with which I took my practical exam. And the same nurse who gave me that critique was one of the testers. The testing committee consists of one nurse from the ward and one nurse from the nurse from the school.

Well thirty minutes have gone by and I still have to go shopping , to the book store - I ordered a book on the Dead Sea Scrolls because they fascinate me, and I have got to go to the post office with this letter"

Parker and the dread

Often Parker felt dread. Like today on God Friday. His emotional bowl of feelings was full on days like this. His daughter was visiting with her husband. He imagined he would spend time with her. Perhaps he would place a board game like Monopoly with her. But when he actually stood before the situation – he could not bring himself to offer to play a game with her. On a day like today there were often guests in the house – so Parker couldn't wear his raggy jogging pants and faded black T-shirts because he looked like a hag in these clothes. He had to wear his jeans and a decent shirt around the house. That was especially bothering when he was sitting at the table or doing clean up in the kitchen. Today his wife had invited her sister and her husband for lunch and in the afternoon his son had several friends over to cook a pizza and have some fun. So he sat at his desk and felt his tight jeans squeezing his fat belly and legs. This made his miserable and added to his general malaise.

Parker had more items on his list of things he wanted to do than there was time in the day. He had 3 books in process and he had a Kindle full of almost fifty books that he fancied himself reading. But Parker was undecided where to start. Parker also had plenty to do in the yard – like sawing and chopping wood, mowing the lawn – but it was a holiday and using loud machines or making the chopping sounds that would bother the neighbors was not allowed on holidays – besides it was raining.

Parker wanted to write a story but after writing a half a page his mind ran blank most of the time. Parker thought he wanted to spend his entire time reading books but evenings he would often watch 2 or three hours television. Parker had also watched television for endless hours as a child. When he came home from school he often sat in the play room from 3:00 P.M on until dinner which his mom or dad made around 7:00 P.M. Then after dinner her had a couple of shows that he wanted to catch. He sat there lots of times until bedtime.

Parker felt he should spend time with his wife or daughter. He had the feeling he should sit together with them but when they were talking about cooking he fled the table to his office. Then he sat there at his desk could not decide whether to read, to write or record to take a nap…

After a while he began to write. That was an exaggeration – he did not know what to write - which made him aware of the dread again. Just filling up the first page seemed to elude him. When dread had overcome him he could not recall. But it had crept up on him over the years. Why? He had been waiting to study German again ever since he came to Germany – what irony. He waited every day of his life for 28 years to finally start his study. Always there had been reasons to prevent him from going to the university again. His wife had always wanted other things and things that took up his time and took up their money. He had waited to study because he dreaded her reaction if he dared to enroll and go to the university on a daily basis. The dread now lived in him. It gave him a tight stomach. It kept him from sleeping well at night. The dread eclipsed the happiness in his life like the clouds and the cold eclipsed the sun on this cold rainy afternoon. Now it seemed to him that his energy level and concentration level had sank so far into the ground that he had no energy for the task – even if he had a few free hours for reading and studying. His waiting had turned into dread. He dreaded that time was running out and he dreaded that he could not make good on 28 years. He dreaded failure. He dreaded and dreaded and dreaded and come to no resolve. This was probably the darkest day of his life.

Parker and the Suffering

This was the issue for Parker. You could go back to 1975 or you could go back to 1995 or again in 2005. The suffering could always be found. Each time Parker had avoided the suffering out of fear. He tried to act like the suffering would go away if he just ignored it long enough. It was fear that kept Parker from moving ahead. Parker feared that if he did what was necessary to remedy the suffering his world would fall apart. Instead he insisted in holding on to the status quo. He feared death.. He feared the process of dying. He feared pain. He feared sickness. He feared the process of getting old. He feared being left alone. He feared failure. He feared and feared. And so he spent his years between fear and denial. He had been doing this ever since he could remember – even as a small child. He has done this as small child when he had his first terrible night mare of being in that gray old alley and being left alone in the car by his mother, or with the fantasy he had as a 4 year old boy, that the Germans (German soldiers) would come to him at night in his bed take him away. To avoid this he imagined himself telling the Germans that he was only a head and therefore not worth taking (he would pull the cover up to his neck – hiding the rest of his body beneath the blanket). In the present day when he wished he could have his own apartment and do what he wanted without his wife complaining about what he was doing – He only did housework or left his office out of fear of her disapproval when he would rather be thinking and writing an listening to music or cassettes. And he suffered because of fear. He tried to hide his fear from himself. Every once in a while he had the courage to call his fear by name and write it down. But writing it down did not make it go away and did not get him out of his dilemma – which seemed to be growing while his youth was disappearing.

He feared he would spend his whole life fearing and therefore suffering.

This letter reminded him that he had always had the answer but never the courage to fix the problem

"Dear John,

Saturday, 30 July 2005

2:15 P.M.

I re-read your letter on pain and suffering. There came more insight out of it than at first glance. I had not made any differentiation between pain and suffering. It shows that you have a keen mind. You should write a book. It is funny but I had the thought that you should write a book and at once a second thought - John is probably writing a book!

The information on the tissue shrinking was like light coming on in a dark room. I had already surmised that, as my back trouble began shortly after I quit nursing - where I heavily used my back daily lifting persons in and out of bed and wheelchairs -, the pains were coming from the fact that I were no longer using the muscles of my back. And, as a result, the muscles were tearing at the vertebrae causing them to "dis-align". I had some trouble in March already in a different spot. But on 6 June when I woke up with my "attack" I suddenly had pain in my mid-back which has continued up until now. The orthopedist - who I do not think is any good - took x-rays and said I had 3 compression fractures in my mid back - B8 and B9 and L1. He said one looked fresh and two looked older. He wanted me to do a nuclear bone scan. (I freaked out -) NO NO - I have not been back to him. I do not want any more visits to the doctor at this time.

I am not suffering about not being to do the physical activities that I used to do. I can walk and ride a bike and I feel great about it. I am suffering in an other area. I listen to often to Hannelore. She feels that since I do not have a career - I should be ashamed of myself - I that I have no hope of ever recovering from this shameful condition.... I have really punished myself with bad thoughts of myself - ever since I have arrived here! Because I did not come equipped with a career - one that I had chosen and pursued with a passion... And nursing was a horrible mistake. I tried to make it work - by doing it so long though it was torturing me. It was rubbing salt into an open wound – causing inflammations in all my deep seated fears of sickness and death. You may think this would have been a great way to overcome such fears - but it was not for me. I failed it if this was supposed to be a test. My suffering comes from not being the person I perceived myself to be 25 years ago. (Never becoming it)

The pains in the body together with the age became the alarm signal to me that time has ticked and is ticking. And at this time I cannot recreate my image of me to fit my life as it has been and may well be. Despair set in. No sign of the positive hope I felt in the times of Jack Boland....

I cannot spend time in thought and contemplation because I am caught in shame and fear.... the rest takes care of itself.

I was deeply moved by your words and will have to return to them again to get all the meaning out of them. They are packed with more that the few lines on the computer could express.

Have a nice day

LOVE Parker"

Parker and "The past is gone and we need to leave it behind"

Parker's mother was 86 years. She had told him to leave the past behind. If she could say this then it must be possible for Parker. That was the problem with looking at old letters and trying to figure out what when wrong in the past. It was hard work. After reading each old letter the weight of the past seems to grow. Still Parker believed he could leave it behind better if he first looked at his whole past again. Parts of his past seemed out of his reach. Since he had come to Germany everything he had experienced before seemed to be forgotten. There were no reminders. No Adrian that could be visited, no Michigan State, No baseball games no Parker family gatherings that he could attend. Yes this time seemed gone. No one in his life now could share these memories with him. Perhaps these memories could have been shared by exchanging letters with his brothers and sisters. He had hoped something like this could have been achieved through the medium of email. But to his hundreds of letters to his family he had gotten only sparsely few in return. And no one in his pas could share his new life and memories. So he had two halves to his life and each half separate from the other and neither could be reconciled with the other. His father had died and that seemed to close the door back into his former life forever. But his mother still lived and although, for him she did not contain the keys to the doors of his past. Her could still write her and call her. This was some advice of hers in a letter that seemed appropriate for his present state of mind and his current project:

Oct 15 1993

.... Parker, your letters are very wonderful and your changing and growing is very evident...

August 18, 1993

... The past is gone and we need to leave it behind and look for new opportunities... of course you can succeed if you choose to and start telling yourself that you are capable.

... Enjoy your time at home and savor it. Don't let anything diminish your pleasure in it... it is important to do well at anything we try. We do not have to try to be loved or respected if we are giving it our best shot.... don't judge your thoughts. Thoughts are just that and are not to be judged, but to be retained or dismissed...

Prophecy

Parker had written years ago to his mother. He was torn then between responsibility and pursuit of his passion. German and religion was his passion then and it was his passion now. Also In one year he had written over 100 letters – He was letter writer. Bit his words had left him… His father had died and his spirit had died when he forced himself to become a nurse. Duty told him you had better do it and fear told him you will loose yourself if you do not finish your training – and that was right he had to finish the nurses training. And he had to suffer to become what he was – but this was at the cost of his happiness and joy and peace of mind and of the most valuable things to him – his past and his freedom and his passion and his roots and his brothers and his sisters and his most terrible pride. He thought to himself… you decide
An as he had written this he felt happy and he felt hope…

"Dear Mom,
13. August 1993

I just took the dog for his morning run in the woods. This morning the sun is shining for the first time in the morning in weeks. It has rained everyday for the past 8 weeks. This morning it rained too but then the sun came out and the beauty of the woods is like a paradise, fresh, moist, green, yellow sun rays peeking through the forest roof. I feel my "alpha waves".

It seems a shame to let such thoughtful moments go by without sharing them with you. The day will be busy. I will be sweeping the sidewalk, mowing the lawn, emptying-cleaning and refilling the pool in which we take a quick morning plunge in every morning.
I do this only occasionally but Hannelore does it every morning.

I will be picking up Daria from school and shopping and then preparing lunch. Today is the beginning of weekend and my 3 ladies will all be here for lunch.

I find the books by Silva to be very interesting and am anticipating the set of tapes!!!

Yesterday I had some thoughts that I wrote down and would like to share with you in short paragraphs that I wrote them in. Here they are:

Here are some candid unfiltered thoughts. Since I have no one here with whom I candidly speak I am sending you these thoughts. What I would like from you is not to judge these as good or bad but to look as them and see which ones are logical. And which ones reveal and unbalanced point of view that would not bear any fruitful results in the manifest world of our "demonstrations"(A Jack Boland term).

My outlook on life is different now. I have bound myself into a family structure and lost my personality,(my integrity?)
Did I predict this in 1975 when I wrote, "Conformity's demands club him into senselessness and rejection of his integrity of mind?"

If I had to do it over again I would stay at the university and get my master's degree in German and then apply to another university and get my doctorate. I would worry about money and property so I could be free to study German, and other languages and perhaps bible scriptures. I was interested in the Gnostic gospels and where the writings of the other apostles went to. Also I would like to know what other historical details are recorded of events that took place in Middle East around the time of "Jesus".

I don't know if I can be a nurse but I must try and hopefully succeed. My mother can find out for me if the German training is recognized in the U.S.

Birthdays: If I send my mother money then I she could buy a present for me and give it to the person having birthday.

Dad: I could send dad cards occasionally that he could show to his customers and brag about his son living in Germany - something he could fun with. I could send him money and ask him to open and American bank account for me then I could save for the move back to America. I think it is time for me to go back when I have finished my training.

Car: Who could loan me money to buy a car? How would I pay this money back?

In my letters to family members I have dialoged with each of my brothers and sisters and mom and dad. These are the subjects I discuss with them:
Mom: spiritual things.
Dad: money and on being a father- my dad says I am stubborn and intelligent like my mother.
Nancy: mental and psychological questions and questions on family matters and raising a family
Jean: her family and Steve's business
Joe: brotherly things and about his family and Mary
John: we discuss the world and our struggles in life.
Cathy: teaching problems, religious things and her and Kevin's life

Marti: we discuss family matters, her problems in her daily life and her and Kerry's relationship.

This time at home is good time and I am gather spiritual strength and confidence in myself. I am learning to know myself again. Thoughts come to me and I do not deny them.

Training as a nurse: I must do this training and begin serving people. I have avoided my responsibility too long and I have found no real peace. I still want to learn more German but this must be done now as a later hobby and perhaps one day when I have served enough I can then do this German as a profession. What is the answer to this dilemma? This is what I would like to know with certainty from the Universal Creative Intelligence. Hannelore's mother says that many of her friends say that they think that I perfectly suited to be a nurse. Hannelore's father says that it is important that I do a good job and am loved and respected by the people I care for and people in general. I wonder what my mother would say to this.

Well that is all for now I have got lots to do. Love Jim. "

Parker and the Marriage agreement

Later on that morning, after offering a divorce to his wife, Parker sat there at the computer editing an old letter he had written 20 years ago, (She had not accepted his offer – although he had been hoping secretly to finally get time to read and write during the evenings. He thought of all the hours that he had until now spent, evening for evening, for the past 28 years at her side watching TV or vacuuming and tidying the house because it put her in a good mood. He would be free and he would be move into a hole or dump, which was all he would be able to afford with the pocket money her earned at the call center – but he would be free). He and his wife had discussed her need to have a marriage agreement that would protect her if he ever decided to run off with another a woman just because she had offered him good sex. It was absurd. He had been thinking with fear in his heart and hope for his new beginning for two days about how to explain to her that her money was not important to him. On the other hand if she was going to die on him then he could not agree that she was not willing to leave him the house in her will.

31 Jan 1993

*"Last week I wrote Mom a letter in which I reflected upon the first several months that I was in Germany. As I write this I almost have to laugh - because I haven't accomplished much since I have been here but I am extremely satisfied about having been here. I have regretted much but somehow I have enjoyed it. I have learned to forget the days that I have cursed my ever coming here and I remember the fun and interesting moments! (Daria is playing happily and busily in the room where I am typing this. Her cheerful singing is heart warming to me - it gives me a real feeling of joy. This entire weekend she has been putting her entire stock of puzzles together. The whole floor was spread out with puzzles. She has kept herself busy for hours. Now she just put all here puzzles away and sang a song about herself doing it as she was doing it. And I think **WOW! HOW WONDERFUL!**) - so back to the subject*

As I looked thru all the letters that I have received since I have come here I read about all the events that took place in 1984 and 1985. - You got married, Marti and Cathy graduated from high school, and there were several great family parties. I really began to feel remorse at having missed all this and I got the feeling for a few moments that the time had come to pack my bags and head for Michigan. Of course - the clock cannot be turned back.

If you knew what was waiting on you then would you have gotten married and still lead your life in the same direction? I would have. Sure I would like to have accomplished certain things that I have not but - I do not regret where I have been and I am now. But looking to the past - looking at old newspaper articles about the sports events, the plays and musicals and the musical groups I have been in - and reading old letters and looking at pictures of old girlfriends that I had- which I was doing today helped me to remember - my pride - which I have swallowed 100s of times since I have been with Hannelore and since I have been a father- "

Parker winced at this passage. He had not only swallowed his pride but he had vomited it out too. And this he had done thousands of times.

Parker and not doing the things he wanted to do

It was clear to Parker many years ago that he was abusing himself by not following his own desires. He should have left his wife after the first week of living in Germany. He was very sure about his duty as father to Gesa and too blind to the danger of never saying no to his wife. Then one day the great store of patience, love and hope he had brought with him was drained out. He was extremely durable in his constitution. He had had enough even then in 2000. But it took him almost 4 more years until he broke. That is when he quick working as a nurse. He had hoped it would help him save his soul. But he went on taking the verbal beatings of his wife and went on being afraid to go back to the USA or go to the Oldenburg University – and though he was broken he continued on. He couldn't function as a nurse anymore but he did function as a houseman for 17 months. He did not get any thanks for this from his wife. Instead he got only disrespect and anger.

So that when the day came that he me Manuela in the program for the reintegration program offered to him by the Employment office, he could not resist her friendliness. Her affection was like cool water for a thirsty plant in a hot dry desert. She told him she felt like she had known him for ever and that she had a special intuitive connection with him. This was too much to resist. And they enjoyed each others company for 6 weeks. It was spring. All of nature was fresh and green. They walked along dikes and along the shore of the sea. They went out to the movies and to dinner. They spent every break together during the 6 weeks of the program before they were sent into their new jobs, For Parker it was the sweetest time he had had since he came to Germany. She was young and attractive and liked to go places and have fun. It was for Parker to this day a time he fondly remembered. For the first time in 20 years almost he was doing the things he wanted to do.

"01 June 2000

I have spent years here - not doing the things I want to do.

Of course - it is my own choice. I am not talking about studying

at college right now. (That is another issue) I am talking about

all the time I spent in front of the TV screen these years.

Tonight I wrote a letter on the computer while the family was

watching TV. I am proud of myself. You know that I like

languages and literature.(some literature) I want to learn many of them.

I have spent so much time watching TV with Hanni...

I want to be near her too... But I am not happy doing this.

Living as a bachelor would not have fulfilled me either. It

is just that Hanni has demanded too much time over the years.

I am just getting to the point where I don't feel the need

to have her approval all the time. I have nagged her with

enough complaints now since I have been nursing - that she has

sort of gotten the message - ."

Manuela was also married and neither Parker nor she was ready to really end their marriages with their partners. So that after the partners found out about their dates there was open anger and sadness in both marriages. Parker and Manuela stopped seeing each other. Manuela later divorced her husband. She had no children that kept them together for other reasons. Parker stayed together with his wife because she wanted him to stay. It would have been difficult anyway to separate because both Parker and his wife did not want the complications that divorce with children brings.

Parker and the run in the woods

Spring 1993

This morning while I was running in the woods, I saw that the sun is shining for the first time in the morning in weeks. It has rained everyday for the past 8 weeks. This morning it rained too but then the sun came out and the beauty of the woods is like a paradise, fresh, moist, green, yellow sun rays peeking through the forest roof. I feel my "alpha waves". It seems a shame to let such thoughtful moments go by without sharing them with you. The day will be busy. I will be swee-ping the sidewalk, mowing the lawn; emptying cleaning and re-filling the pool in which we take a quick morning plunge in every morning. I do this only occasionally but Hannelore does it every mor-ning. I will be picking up Daria from school and shopping and then preparing lunch. Today is the beginning of weekend and my 3 ladies will all be here for lunch. I find the books by Silva to be very interesting and am anticipating the set of tapes!!!   Yesterday I had some thoughts that I wrote down and would like to share with you in short paragraphs that I wrote them in.

Here they are: Here are some candid unfiltered thoughts. Since I have no one here with whom I candidly speak I am sending you these thoughts. What I would like from you is not to judge these as good or bad but to look as them and see which ones are logical. And which ones reveal and unbalanced point of view that would not bear any fruitful results in the manifest world of our "demonstrations"(A Jack Boland term). My outlook on life is different now. I have bound myself into a family structure and lost my personality,(my integrity?)   Did I predict this in 1975 when I wrote, "Conformity's demands club him into senselessness and rejection of his integrity of mind." If I had to do it over again I would stay at the university and get my master's degree in German and then apply to another university and get my doctorate. I would worry about money and property so I could be free to study German, and other langua-ges and perhaps bible scriptures. I was interested in the Gnostic gospels and where the writings of the other apostles went to. Also I would like to know what other historical de-tails are recorded of events that took place in Middle East around the time of "Jesus". I don't know if I can be a nurse but I must try and hopefully succeed. My mother can find out for me if the German training is recognized in the U.S. birthdays: If I send my mother money then I she could buy a present for me and give it to the person having birthday. Dad: I could send dad cards occasionally that he could show to his customers and brag about his son living in Germany something he could fun with. I could send him money and ask him to open and American bank account for me then I could save for the move back to America. I think it is time for me to go back when I have finished my training. Car: Who could loan me money to buy a car? How would I pay this money back?

Perhaps I should learn to seek God first, follow and respect his principle first and then Hannelore would respect me. I like the Book of James in the Bible. It has a lot of good advice and sayings that I can follow. Unemployment: I have been enjoying my unemployment like a va-cation. It gives me time to remember my values and write let-ters to my family. Hannelore sees her mother and sisters everyday!!! Her time with them she takes for granted. I would too if I lived among my brothers and sisters. I feel that she can-not even conceive of what I mean when I tell her this. This time at home is good time and I am gather spiritual strength and confidence in myself. I am learning to know my-self again. Thoughts come to me and I do not deny them. Training as a nurse: I must do this training and begin serving people. I have avoided my responsibility too long and I have peace. I still want to learn more German but this must be done now as a later hobby and perhaps one day when I have served enough I can then do this German as a pro-fession. What is the answer to this dilemma? This is what I would like to know with certainty from the Universal Creative Intelligence. Hannelore's mother says that many of her friends say that they think that I perfectly suited to be a nurse. Hannelore's father says that it is important that I do a good job and am loved and respected by the people I care for and people in general. I wonder what my mother would say to this. Well that is all for now I have got lots to do.

Love Parker

Parker and the Boredom at Condor

Saturday, 13 February 2010

Yesterday was Marti's birthday. I did not send her a card.

Getting up in the morning is hard. I would like to get up at 6:00 but then I would probably get tired by 9:00 again. Hannelore is sleeping in the guest room. I hear her snoozing.
She and Carl watched a movie until way after midnight. I was falling asleep so I went to bed.

I have been fidgeting in bed since 6:00. Tossing and turning and worrying about how Hannelore is going to get to school this week. There is still snow and ice all over the place and she will not be pleased at the prospect of walking.

We could use another car – but we are so far in debt with the credit card that there is not another penny to spare. Carl needs 80 British pounds, and new shoes and 100 Euros for his birthday. That is another 300 Euros on the card. That means there is around 4500 on the card this month. That is the most up until this point.

The weeks go by and I cannot remember one day for the next.

What did I do Monday? (Before work) ??????

Yesterday… The usual routine… got up .. made coffee… took Carl to Zetel to the bus stop…had a cup of coffee… took Hannelore to school…on the way there … I suggested she borrow a car…. or whatever I cannot remember exactly… and she got loud and told me something like … she is tired of having to rely on other people and so on … this gets me emotionally upset … I feel she blames me for all of her money problems….

That was our ride to school. We had a typical discussion that we have had almost everyday since I quit nursing. All I want to so in this situation is escape to a better relationship with someone else… but I do not because… there is no one else and it would make life too messy.

Before going to work I fed the chickens, I picked up the house and swept and mopped. I made phone calls to the Gemeinde about Carls ID card and about the trash collection taxes. I ordered 80 pounds for Carl and called the school and left a message for Hannelore. Then it was already time for work. On the way to work I stopped at Heipis and picked up the salt I had paid for two days ago.

So on the rest of the mornings from Monday to Thursday I did similar things like quick shopping and bank business and shovelling snow and doing laundry and mopping the floor and so on... but I cannot remember the exact details...... and the exact order in which I did what before each day of work. Two times when I got to work I parked directly in front of the entry in order to get there on time. Then after I reported in and logged in on the computer I went back out and parked the car on the big parking lot.

At work I processed Condor emails part of the time every day... To pass the time in between call I made a few scratch papers by ripping the din A 4 papers into 4 sections. This is my activity to fight boredom. I know it is pitiful but it works well to fight back boredom. It is the only activity that I can do in between calls that does not take any concentration and can be interrupted without and loss of the previous effort exerted. If I try to read or write anything and the phone rings (like it does every minute) then I loose track of what I have read or the stream of thoughts I was working on.

Life, my life is so routine or boring... that it seems senseless. I have been considering what I could do to make it exciting... the only thing that occurs to me is to write... to write about a life .... my life... how it would be if it were not so mundane and senseless.

I am really lost.... I was never found... even before I met Hannelore... but I have not gotten any more on track since I have lived here..... I am lost ... far away from any path that I could ever find meaningful... I have no hope of ever finding meaning... and yet I continue down the path I have taken...because of a sense of duty... and of fear.

My whole life has been ruled by fear…dreadful fear….fear of sickness and death yes… but also a fear behind that …If I am honest … I do not have a name for that fear… I could try to give it a name or describe it… but most of what I would say would be stammering meaningless attempts to look at something without achieving clarity….

I am so afraid of the word NO that I just do not ask….

9:29 A.M.

Parker and - The path I tread

Adrian, October 1975

The path I tread I must clear again for myself; for it is seldom traveled.

This bold trek is as bold as Boldness itself.

This way is different than the ruddy roads followed by common men.

On this path there is great danger for the soul.

The mind can stray from order and clear perception.

The heart can be ripped open.

But the ways of common men can punish the spirit, causing the lonely man to lose his spirit.

The ways of men leave his sprit weak like an old tree, robbed of its firmness by insects.

Like the tree, the spirit snaps and falls in the autumn storms.

What do I dream of myself as?

Do I dream of myself as a philosopher, a pianist or a writer?

Do I have the wisdom to know wisdom?

The lonely man stands alone on the lonely highway.

In this life of mine I must follow my own path.

It is not cleared by others.

I shall endure and keep following my heart.

"And the glory of the Lord shall be revealed" by Handel

Adrian, November 1975

What is Beauty?

What is Wisdom?

What is greatness?

How can I be sure of the truth?

What are my true virtues?

Why do I have these questions?

Could it be because I am still growing?

Will these questions go unanswered for me?

Will the misery and uncertainty I am feeling chase me all my life?

Follow your own values.

How do I know my values are true?

,,Then one day there came the end.

The perverse, the pure, the wicked, the wonderful, the suffering, the serenity,

the light, the darkness, all of man's inventions, his games and his thoughts were

resolved. His shame swept away and replaced by love.

This love was the essence of the being who exists in all things.

Adrian, December 1975

What makes me unpleasant to others?

Could it be my face?

I used to think it was my only my face

What is it?

Today was Mr. Shaw was "unpleased" with me.

Mr. Shaw asked me why I seemed so distracted in class.

The only answer I could think of was that I was worried about my complexion and breath odor.

I just clam up when I am worried about this.

I want to get out of the room.

They say if you cannot handle your problems you try to escape by using drugs.

You may start smoking or drinking excessively.

You may become mentally ill.

You may become criminal and begin to steal or do other unpleasant things.

I escape by finding confusion in everything. Or becoming "distracted"

I guess this belongs to the category of mental illness.

Will the misery and uncertainty I am feeling chase me all my life?

The Dilemma

Parker is being forced to write a story by his daughter. This is a terrible dilemma…so.

The belief that no project will ever be finished had long ago taken complete grip of his feelings. It was a matter of pride and a matter of this … - "what else was to be inherited if not a story – and still better - a story that could be sold and make money." At the present Parker was much too poor to leave his kids any money. Parker should have been making more money all along anyway. He remembered his dad's failure at business. Parker's dad had failed in business before Parker was even able to write his name on a piece of paper. How could Parker succeed under circumstances like these? His dad's brother in law had a successful business. He did not go broke. And as a result they had the better houses, the better cars and his kids went to better schools. And to make the point – Uncle Billy always brought his old shoes and old pants and shirts and donated them to Parkers father.

Then later in Germany – Parker never made any money in Germany either. And Parker's sister and brother in law, Karin and Heinrich, were the "Uncle Billy" of Parker's German life. They always had the better jobs, homes and cars everything. They were always bringing old TVs, Computers, furniture and clothes for his wife over to Parkers house – because Parker and his wife had not enough money to buy these things for themselves. Parker had just about had enough of this nonsense. Everybody was making more money   than him. Parker's wife was having a marriage contract drawn up to unsure that he did not get any of the goods that she had amassed since he had been living with her like used TVs and Computers. This was the absolute pits and he cursed the day he ever moved together with her.

Parker had cooked soup for lunch. His wife had suggested pancakes but that had not appealed to him this morning. His soup was too sharp and too salty and she only ate half a bowl. The strawberries he has lovingly bought were too hard and not sweet enough. And at the same time his daughter was there and she had been discussing her brother's drivers training – It was very expensive in Germany – Actually no one had the money to spear for this but it had to be achieved. Parker's son had applied for a job at the supermarket stocking shelves – but this would not start for 2 or 3 weeks and up until now not a penny had been earned by him toward his 2000 Euro expensive drivers training. Therefore Parker's wife was disappointed by lunch and immensely angry at being asked to pay for the drivers training before her son had even earned a cent. Parker felt like a dip shit because with his salary at the call center he could not pay for anything extra – he could contribute maybe 80 Euros per month. That was not nearly enough to pay for the drivers training.

And the whole day had been a drag because the weather was dreary and he would have to return to work tomorrow after being on sick leave. The whole idea of going back to work had left Parker with a feeling of trepidation. He really wished he would never have to go back again.

Parker's wife went to bed angry after lunch with no word of thanks. It always hurt Parkers feelings when she went to take a nap and did not invite him. The day before she had also not invited him to take a nap with her – Still he had gone up to their room to take a nap. Then very shortly he had been rudely awakened with the comment , "You're snoring! "This was because he had a cold and could not breathe through his nose. So - all in all - he was thinking how wonderful it was to be here and be married to his wife.

Parker- Stina an The Earthquake and The Cell Phone

Stina was the younger sister of a friend of Parker's in high school. She was definitely a sweet girl. If he had had more time and more confidence he may have ended up his life living with Stina. Parker liked her then and he liked her later at Michigan State University. Stina was studying there at the same time that Parker was there. In high school Parker took a trip with Stina's family to their cottage in the north. Parker had a little affair with Stina during this trip. But neither Stina nor Parker wanted to make it serious after the trip. They just remained friends and kept there little adventure to themselves. Later at Michigan State during a lonely period for both of them they both secretly played with the idea of getting together with. Somehow the chemistry just wasn't strong enough to hold them together. Still years after, Parker thought of her from time to time and onetime he wrote her an email. He had located her with Internet Service that helped you meet up with old friends from high school. Parker had seen that she was a member but would have had to sign up and pay a fee to contact her. He had decided to let it be. But Stina saw his entry and actually bought a membership just so she could contact him again. Parker was flattered. They exchanged a few letters but nothing ever came out of it. After a while no more emails were exchanged.

Stina,

it sounds likc I am talking to a girl that has been living there all her life. "Earth Quake Preparedness" That sounds like waiting for the final hour.

But do not mind me. I am just a man of little experience in earthquakes. In theory - earth quakes can happen anywhere. (I am thinking my sentence in German first and then translating it into English - I have been here to long. Speaking English is like riding a bike after twenty years of not doing it. It feels good - but I have to get used to the bike.)

It is Sunday and what am I doing? I just cleaned the bathroom and vacuumed the up stairs and I am going to change the bed sheets and covers now. It is crazy. My wife read Harry Potter 7 yesterday and until 4:30 A.M. this morning. I stayed up with her. I got back up at 10 and took the dogs for a walk. I think I feel better when I get less sleep sometimes. Yesterday I was so so so so tired all day long - and I had enough sleep too!

What is the Hayward Fault? Is it named after Rita Haywood - (bad joke)

I made my kids crack up yesterday by acting like I was talking on my cell phone in a busy shopping area. I noticed several people „having conversations with themselves" and I thought - so this is what the world has come to. In former times they would have locked these people up for acting that way. But it gives you a lot of freedom. Just put a fake cell phone in your hand and "scratch your ear" or just hold you hand on your ear- can anyone see if there is a cell phone under there? Then you can talk about anything - and people tolerate it!!

The news about the rest of the family sounds good. Have Greg and Steve had any challenges that could compare to yours? Your love for music really moves me. My daughter would probably love to get to know you. She would oh so much love to sing in choir of the caliber of yours! There are none in our area. I would be interested in recording of your choir.

I called your house on Saturday around 9:30 your time. Your answering machine was on. Was that your voice? It sounded very young. What year and month and date were you born?

Thanks for listening to my "morning". I have needed to talk about my situation for a long time but I am a bit isolated from trustworthy people out of my past. I had one friend from high school, Terry Smith and one friend from college, Matt Burton, but I lost track of them and cannot find them any more. Terry Smith lives in Adrian - but we simply have no contact anymore. I do not know where Matt is and cannot find him.

I would like to tell you more about me and get deeper into where you have been if we can ever find time to exchange this over the computer. I have been so busy today and now it is very late and Hannelore is already in bed and I must not stay up too long or I will disturb her much needed sleep when I come barging into the room. She is 6 years older - born in 1953. She is a high powered person and gives 110 percent to her principle job and is really stressed out at this time of year - just before school gets out on the 19th of July.

I am on vacation. I picked up the house, walked the dogs, and cooked chicken and rice for lunch. (It did not taste good to Hannelore - I hate to cook and mostly ruin any meal I try to prepare. Daria was her too - We did a short video film of her silk screen samples. They are zebras - and she covered them with sand and then blew away with a hair dryer - gradually uncovering them. And as background music the song "A Horse with no Name" It looks quite professional. (Daddy Proud again)

I am listening to KUSP 88.9 Central Coast Public Radio in the Bay Area.

Got to go

JIM

Parker and It never rains in California

He had been looking for something, for any thing that would bring back a feeling he had been missing for a long time. For seventeen months he had been locked up in his houseman existence. His wife was not thankful for his cooking, cleaning, shopping and taxi service. She was just the opposite of thankful. She said, "You're a loser. You will never amount to anything"- She would never forgive him for quitting nursing. Parker was no match for his wife. Parker even believed his wife but it was still terrible to hear her words every day. Parker thought to himself, "If we didn't have children I would have left her long ago. Parker felt like she was a wicked witch and she had enchanted him and locked him up in a cage that he could never escape. Then he met Manuela. She was 17 years younger - he felt joy again! It was that feeling!

He loved the feeling - But Parker was married - and he was a father. No way out! Manuela was married too. His wife had already been someone else's wife too. He paid for that – being the second husband he had been like buying a used car with stained seats scratches in the paint. It was as if his wife had blamed him for everything that had gone wrong in her first marriage. It would be ridiculous to make that mistake again. But had had fallen for Manuela. He would never have broken off with Manuela if she had not stopped their meetings herself. Had had not called Manuela for months - but one afternoon he called her back and she said, "What do you want?" He said, "I will not call you again if you do not want me to." She said that is what she wanted. That was it. She stuck to it. He wrote her letters and drove by her house - Not a single response ever came from her again. That was in the winter of the last year. It had been the most beautiful spring he had had in 23 years. – And it was the worst winter of his life. His sadness at losing her was even worse than his sadness at loosing Julie 28 years ago. Then he was young - then he left for California. The weather was wonderful and he was young and he was going to see his cousin whom he had a crush on. And even when his cousin wanted nothing to do with him - still he was young and he was in California. It never rained that winter and the sun was shinning everyday. It rained every day last winter - he was 47 and on blood pressure medicine and the sun never shined. It never rained in California but it always rains in Germany.

Parker and Another day in poverty

Another day went by for Parker. He was not any farther with his life than he was in June 1977 when he started writing about himself in the third person. He had never ever gotten a real job that he had loved. He had done nursing for a few years but he was a hypochondriac and he was scared to death about his own health facing all the ailments of the human body and soul every nursing day of his life. And what was worse was that he could not leave those nursing experiences behind himself – even after 7 years out of nursing. He was reading a letter from May 95 in which he obviously was not being honest with his father about his early nursing experiences – he hated changing dressings and giving enemas…

Dear Dad

This weekend I have off after working 12 days in a row. I am very happy about that. I am working on a surgical ward still until my vacation on June 19th. Then I have 4 weeks vacation. I am doing a lot of neat kind of nursing work nowadays like dressing the wounds of the people who have been operated on, catheterization, administering enemas, removing stitches and clamps and so on. Work has been interesting lately…

Okay but every thing in that letter was not a complete lie or disaster…

Carl is really a big boy now. He talks to us like a grown up. He can say mom and papa and Gesa and Daria and "laddeh" for chocolate and meow and ruff-ruff and "tele" for telephone and no and and he can wave good-bye and say "oh-oh" for bad behavior. His favorite activity is climbing up the stairs and onto chairs. He is and avid climber with strong arms and legs. He still wakes us up at nights but not as often as a few months ago…

But now he was working at a call center and that was so low pay that he now belonged to the lowest paid employees of Germany and he belonged to the group of people considered to be living in "Armut". The English word is poverty. … But the more he racked his brains the less he understood how he was to ever find his way out of this. And so he ended his thoughts reading the passage about Spring, which he always loved and always raised his spirit…

It has been a long month since I sent my last letter. Spring has arrived here. We have had some real warm days; I have mowed the lawn 3 times already.

The woods have blossomed into a green paradise. We planted our potatoes 2 weeks ago and today I planted pumpkin seeds and Hannelore planted green beans and a lot of flowers. We had to put a fence around the pond and around our garden patch because Carl loves to run through the dirt....

Parker and Finding Enjoyment

Parker could not imagine being unhappy for more than 28 years. But this was the case. He could not remember a time since he had been in Germany in which he had enjoyed himself. He remembered that he had only had an enjoyable time in Germany during the short period of 6 weeks when he had met Manuela. During this time he had taken the training program at the BWN as preparation for his "Buchhändler" training. During that time he was free. There had been no fighting and no pressure with Manu. It was a casual, friendly relationship with no commitment and no plans for the future. During those six weeks he had really enjoyed himself. The fun had lasted until Manuela's husband had returned from his tour of duty on the German naval ship. He had been out for several months. She confessed her sentiment towards Parker to her husband right away, and in a drunken bout of anger, her husband had taken a whack at her. The fun was over. At that time she had no intention of getting divorced from her poor husband. Months later, however, after her contact to Parker had been ended, she did separate from her husband sailor. Manuela had been lonely and she had had fun talking to and spending time with Parker. He been really nice to her and she felt that he was a nice man. But the relationship was necessarily short lived because neither Manu nor Parker had room in their lives for a new lover. It had only been possible for them to get to know each other because they were both in the training program together. They could see each other shortly during and after work. It had also been possible for Parker to get away on a weekend or two. He and Manuela visited the Zoo once together and were gone almost all day. The outing was not at all enjoyable. Manuela did not seem too interested in the Zoo.

During the rest of Parkers time in Germany when he wasn't working, his life had consisted of following daily the wishes of his wife. For years he figured that his time would come. In the beginning the goal was to raise the family. There were things to be done. His children had needed him. And it was obvious that there was little time left over for his "hobbies". But gradually time had passed and he had had decisive confrontations with his wife. He knew he had wanted to go to the university to get his degree in Germany. His wife had told him flatly, "If you dare to enroll in the university then I swear to you we are done." Parker had never had the courage to say, "Then so be it my dear – Tschuß." And in those days where he had been without a job she had been so cruel and critical of Parker. In on his darkest day in Germany when he flunked his nursing exam his wife was speechless and she locked herself in her bedroom for three days. She did not come out for three days and did not talk to him the whole time. Parker's already wounded heart was broken. This was the event that really killed his affection for his wife. But he could not leave his wife because he did not know what to do and did not want to make his children sad. So he stayed on in the marriage. But the joy in his life was gone. He felt had had wasted his time and his chances of happiness had been "pissed out the window". He had to think of his father in this moment. His father had often used that phrase. His father had also told him what a fool he was for chasing after "that woman". His father had said, "German women are tough bitches". And he made a gesture of pounding his fist into his hand. And his Father said, "That is how she will treat you. I meet a lot of German women out on the farms where I sell insurance and they are mean." Two men in Parker's life had prophesized to him at important moments of decision. They were his father and his football coach. He football coach told him he would regret quitting football in the tenth grade – and Parker had regretted it for many years to come. His father had told him he would regret chasing after "that women" and Parker thought to himself very often, "How right my father was in his character analysis of those "German women". Parker had not been equipped to deal with the choices he had made but he had also been too stubborn to take the advice of wise men.

So Parker had thrown away his chances for enjoyment in life because he had not read the signals that life had very clearly given him. Parker had unwisely ignored the warnings on his path and had gone unwisely down the path full of heartache and despair. As he sat there reading his old diary entry from 1976 it all seemed so clear and silly.

"January 1976

I love handwriting and when I write in here I practice my handwriting. Also I try to make my diary interesting. There is stuff in here I would not want anyone to read. It might embarrass me. Maybe people would think I am a rat, a selfish person or even a bad person. In spite of this I hope someday someone will read my dairy and find it interesting.

I wish I could play an instrument very well or paint a picture like an artist. And I wish playing and instrument and painting pictures would be easy for me.

Most of all I want to find enjoyment in my life. I want to be at peace with myself and be happy - which I have never been.

I want to be a whole human being. I want to paint a picture of life around me, write the most interesting story and compose the most enjoyable music. I would like to be the perfect person. Alas, I am far from any of these things.

January the 4th, 1976 – 10:12 P.M.

Today was the first day of sunshine this year.
The skies were clear. Not a cloud. The temperature is about 18 degrees Fahrenheit. Tomorrow Christmas vacation is over and it is back to school. I am tired of all this free time so it is good to get back to school. We have exams in 2 weeks. Maybe that will keep me busy and I can force myself to study and review a little bit each day.

If I study for a couple of hours every day the preparations for the exams should not be too strenuous and should be able to learn at a leisurely pace. If I proceed like I did today it may be quite an ordeal. Today I did not read, practice the piano or do any home work. I just sat around. At 10:00 A.M. I went to church. Afterwards I had lunch and watched TV. The 6 Million Dollar Man was quite interesting to watch. That was all. So I say good night. What will I do tomorrow?

January the 5th

Outside it is icy cold and the wind is blowing quite strongly. The sky if crystal clear blue laced with fluffy feathery white clouds.

Today I took my piano lessons. I had practiced a lot this week but Istill made mistakes. I did not "get rid "of any song today. But maybe my attitude is wrong. Maybe I should not try to "get rid" of songs. I should enjoy a song as long as my teacher thinks I need to practice it. I should be happy to have a chance to get better and better at a song. Only when you have mastered a song technically is it possible to make music.

I am also making slow progress at learning to play the violin. I do not practice a lot and besides it is more difficult than I thought it would be. I cannot expect to be perfect overnight.

The first day back at school was just the same as usual. I am tired. I shall go to bed.
Tomorrow I need to buy some stationary so I can write letters again. Goodnight.

January 6th.
I got a few minutes before we eat. So I am writing my diary to use the time constructively. Today the sky was crystal clear and it was 20°degree Fahrenheit – very cold outside but it had been even colder yesterday.

I felt like shit this morning. I was very sluggish and therefore got out of the house late. The sun was just bringing light to the horizon. The morning clouds were resting on the horizon and tinted the sky a lovely pink and blue. The light was a radiant and unprintable yellowish orange which filled the gaps between the clouds the sun was just out of sight below the horizon. As I walked along I was lost in concentration. Then I become aware of the biting cold around my nose and mouth. As I glanced back at the horizon the radiant glory of the light had faded in a dull gray. For a while I paid no attention to the sky but as I reached the school I glanced again at the horizon. The dull gray had changed yet again into an impressive golden orange and red wave of radiance. I cannot image it ever being possible to capture the beauty of this living sky in a painting. A painting is static but the sky is a chameleon that is ever changing its shape and colors. This living light of the sky is painted with God's colors and far too magic to ever be captured by the hand of a human painter.

Well… dinner is ready…

Dinner was okay. But I should eat slower because I stuffed myself much to full. Joe and I did the dishes voluntarily. That is the biggest miracle on earth. However, we did have our disagreements. But I really cannot remember what they were.,

One thing I have noticed about me and my brother is that we both seemed to have a change of heart lately. Both of us seem more willing to help out around the house more now than before. We both are more amicable to everyone in the house – except of course towards each other. Joe still thinks I am a selfish little baby. I am a bit selfish – but no more selfish that he is. He still picks on me. Well… I will try harder to be nicer to him.

After the dishes I practiced more or less diligently the piano. It was poor practice. I kept falling asleep at the keyboard. I had to get up to close the door because someone was fighting outside, dogs were howling, cats were wining and the roof was falling off and snow was coming in…the part about the cats and dogs is not true. I thought it sounded funny though.

It was rotten practice."

Parker And The Gnostic Gospels – And The Matrix

Parker was 19 when he first heard of the Gnostic Gospels. He was a camp counselor at Camp De Sales in the Irish Hills. In the staff library located in the common room for camp counselors he picked up an old crusty book with the simple title "The Gnostic Gospels". How could it be? Could the church have suppressed this information all this time? This was not part of catechism? The fairy tale of Jesus that the church teaches was not so certain after all. Since then Parker had been interested in finding out the truth about it. The Gnostic Gospels showed that the Jesus portrait that was handed to Catholics was a biased portrait handed down by a Church that was more interested in holding its monopoly to the keys to the kingdom of heaven than it was in the pursuit of truth and goodness. So now Parker had been awoken out of the "Matrix" There was more to know than traditional New Testament that the Church had created. It was up to him to find out. For Parker this became a life long journey. In this letter Parker tells his sister about a part of his journey.

"Hello Nancy,

Thanks for the letter. It is Sunday 7:15 A.M. - I woke up at 6:00 - like clock work. I always take a ramipril 10mg pill at six on week days and most of the time I wake up on weekend at 6:00 sharp - and I know that the dogs are waiting to be taken out so my conscience will not let me sleep peacefully any way - unless I am exhausted - besides the fresh air of the woods always does my system good - I always wake up with a kind of tension - like I could climb out of my skin or like a tension in my breast - no pain or other symptoms - just tension - It dissolves itself however while I am out on the fresh air for 20 minutes in the woods.

I am really fighting with my weight right. I wake up one morning at 103 kilogram and the next 101 kilogram - I need to get under the weight of 100 kilograms! I can tolerate 101 because it is on its way to 100 but when I wake up with 103 - after a day of hardy eating I get a sort of panic - I say - watch out - your arteries won't reward you for that kind of load. On those days it would be better not to weigh myself - because I worry about it all day and I cannot change it anyway.

It is a good thing there are flu shots - because otherwise a lot of people would get the flu and really suffer. Hannelore got her shot already - I would like one but I don't like to go to the doctor.

Hannelore and Carl have two weeks fall vacation and I have to work 2 weeks 43.75 hours. That is 6.25 hours overtime per week or in these 2 weeks 12.5 hours overtime. I may be able to get one day a week off for the rest of the year starting the 2nd week in November - that is what I am hoping for. Hannelore is in a sour mood because I never do cleaning at night when I come home from work. I refuse to - cleaning is for me a waste of "life's time" I do not mind cleaning - but with 2 dogs, a kid and a wife at home - (especially the dogs - because of dirt) and (especially the messiness because of the kid and wife) the place does not stay clean even for 24 hours - so it seems senseless to go through the same cleaning routine every day when I have so little time anyway - I refuse to do that anymore - but Hannelore makes life miserable otherwise anyway with her nagging - then she cleans a little herself but leaves the vacuum cleaner laying right in he middle of the room when she is finished or she changes her bed sheets but leaves mine alone - this is the absolute insult - even if I were mad an I changed the bed sheets I would change hers too any way. I can ignore the nagging for a few days but after a period of time it does get tome through the back door affecting my mood anyway. And the culmination is then her cleaning frenzies - pushing everyone and everything aside wile she is cleaning and she has the big loud screeching sign on her for head - you are all worthless dipshits because you won't clean - now watch me do it!!

So I suppose I don't need to wonder where my tension comes from do I??

It is all best to endure with 5mg diazepam (I think they call that valium)

Okay - I am leaving that path of thought for the moment and changing the subject. I have been really into reading about the origins of the Christian religion. I have read about 4 or 5 books about the subject after reading The Da Vinci Code. I had been interested in the Gnostic and Coptic gospels anyway before the Dan Brown book anyway. I am reading a book called "The Jesus Dynasty. The Hidden History of Jesus" by James D. Tabor - Professor at the University of North Carolina in Charlotte N.C.

He investigates several interesting possibilities like Jesus' father being a Roman named Panthera - who then died later in the Germany serving in the Roman Army - The father's full name Tiberius Julius Abdes Pantera whose grave stone exists near Bad Kreuznach in Germany. He says Jesus was probably not a carpenter but a stone mason and that Joseph died early Mary was married to his brother named Klopas. Who probably died early too leaving Jesus as the oldest to support Mary and his brothers and sisters by working in his profession as a "tekton" which means handworker - The wood industry was not booming in the region where not all to many trees existed besides olive and fig trees. And Jesus could have worked in a nearby city (now only ruins) called Sepphoris where Herodus was rebuilding his King's residence. So it is very interesting intriguing material - it is as interesting as vantasy or science fiction - even though it is only a dry non fiction popular science book.

Daria wants me to write a fiction novel - about Jesus or Maria Magdalena - maybe - I realize however that it is just too much work - But her are the first few words of the unfinished novel (translated - because I wrote them in German)

- It was urgent and Jesus had to hurry! Something had gone wrong. Lazarus had not come out. It was now almost 4 days ago now. Jesus had led him into the cave - the ritual underworld. Lazarus was to born again and then journey to Egypt with Jesus to enter the Closter of the Sacred Feminine. But the Lazarus had not come out and the women had sent news to him. It arrived much too late. It was getting late and the Sun gleamed red on the horizon. There was nothing left of the warmth of the afternoon sun. The coolness was everywhere and it cooled the sweat on Jesus brow. In less than an hour the orange sphere would sink beneath the mountains horizon and the Lazarus would surely never come out again. The Sabbath would begin and no one would be allowed into the Garden of the dead. The gate would be guarded by the guards of the Priests. As he arrived at the city gates the Roman soldiers barred his way. There had been uprisings in the city and any one trying to flee would be arrested. The Romans were still seeking the rebellions and had closed down all the entries to the city. But Jesus had healed a son of an Roman officer a year before and this officer was on duty at the gates on this evening. He lead Jesus out of the city and released him. Jesus hurried along to the Garden. As he arrived at the Garden the Guards of the Priests was posted already. They warned Jesus. "Master - the sun is setting and we cannot let you pass" Jesus answered, " I am going into the kingdom of the dead where the sun only rises. I will return in 3 days. Until then you will not see me again - therefore let me pass." The guards of the priests knew of the ritual of the dead. They did not believe that Lazarus had succeeded because he had not come out the evening before. But Jesus spoke with urgency and they had pity on Lazarus so they let Jesus pass. They locked the gates and let no one else pass that Sabbath.

Well - that is all for now -

LOVE Parker"

Parker and Mary

When I was little everything around me was big and seemed so large. Everything seemed to be twice as large as it now appears to me. And now, the size of most things, like tables, chairs, porch steps and the size of the house in general, do not impress me. They so not seem overlarge anymore. Seeing thins this way is like taking the excitement out of life. It is like they left the spice of life out or the salt out of the bread of life.

The older I get the more changes I undergo. When I was little I imagined leading a heroic life. I imagined being happy and having an adventure every day of my life. I imagined the scenario "boy meets girl and they live happily ever after" The boy was to work hard and become famous. Life was supposed to be given to me on a silver platter. The reality of the life I am leading is altogether different than I expected. The rules of life are changing and if I want to live up to my expectations of myself I will have to change things. (I know I should never have quit the football team.)

Chapter 3 of my life's story:

I do not remember much of my baby years when we lived on Carlton Road. Some of the images are still very vivid. The images are mostly ones of fear of the neighbor's large dog and of being abandoned on the porch steps by my parents and of fearing the tornado that we were watching from our basement window during a summer storm. I remember a bit more about life in our house on Maumee Street. I remember becoming aware of how to twist a few rules and get what I want. I remember becoming aware of being alone - separate from all others. I began to see my mom and dad fight and fear that they would get divorced.

It is late and my hand is getting tired so I will stop writing here. The question remains..., what is the meaning of my life and what lies ahead?
2 January 1976

Today was not a bad day. (It was amazing to me to have a good day.) Today I was thinking about Mary. I think I will write some letters on the weekend practice the piano or maybe read a book.

I picked up my room today. That is amazing and exciting! The church was having a retreat and someone asked me to go but I did not want to because I am not getting along well with the kids of my church right now. There is also no sweet girl that I am interested in there right now. I am still much in love with Mary from Detroit. Unfortunately I cannot get her to be my girlfriend. I am sure I would love her for the rest of my life if she would only commit to me. (There was never any chance that happening)

Monday I have to go back to school. Christmas break is over. Today the weather was cloudy and cold. I spent all day indoors. Now I am going to wash up and hit the sack. I will dream of Mary in Detroit and of Sister Ruth of Siena Heights.

My dream will go like this... stop crying... live... write a letter to Ruth and Mary... it is great... to the end...

I have just visited Mary at her home in Detroit. I believe my heart's crust has been cracked. I felt so close to her during my visit. The wall of isolation that I have built up around me since I was 4 years old seems to have gotten a little tiny crack in it where Mary has reached my heart with hers. She showed me a glimpse of herself and of her family. (The same thing would happen years later with Julie Koelzer - I also visited her in Grand Rapids at her home during a semester break. I would still be much in love with Julie from Grand Rapids if we had stayed together. Now I can recall little of our days together. But I loved Julie much longer than I loved Mary.)But now back to Mary…

Mary of Detroit loves her family so much. She is much more devoted to her family than I have been to mine. She is ready to invest her time and energy in them and misses them dearly when she is away at the Siena Heights High school. I have not missed my family in the least up until now...

Mary gave an old lady in her neighborhood a box of candy. That was such a gesture of love that impressed me. But Mary sees herself through other eyes. I wish I could tell her how much she means to me and how great I think she is. But she would not be impressed by my opinion. Mary is a sort of sad person.

Now that I am home again I have started to "search for my family. I feel that I want to be closer to my parent and siblings.

That seems funny to me but I know this change in heart has been caused by Mary. Mary's love has really moved me to tears almost.

Thank you, Mary. I say to myself, "let me move from the past and begin living in the now moment. I hope this feeling will last and not just be for the moment. I wish Mary and I could be together. My love for her seems so right - but the sadness of separation from her makes me so miserable. She is special for me. But I have to let her live her own life. She will never be part of my life and I have to let her go. I love you Mary. Let your life shine on others as it has on me.

3rd January 1976 2:45 A.M. Good morning and good night.

I love to watch "happy end" movie at this time in my life. I want to believe whole heartedly in the happy end. If I don't start to let people into my heart, if I am always on my guard I will never find a friend and be able to keep her. If I fear getting hurt I could never trust anyone. I would only think people are no good and not concerned about me. I must learn to be happy in the group instead of rather being alone. I must learn to grow from my friendships, accepting the good of them without trying to hold on to tight to the person. People must come and go in my life and friends will leave or be left behind. New friends can only come if I let go the friends who have moved on and are not near me anymore. I should not grieve the loss of onetime girlfriends. I should be truly thankful for the beauty my friends and girlfriends have shown me. I should fondly remember what they have shared with me. And I should move forward and share myself with others.

Parker and his son's friend Michael

So here he was – Parker. So many years later after he departed the USA from the Detroit Airport he was sitting in the house office listening to his son's heavy metal music. The music was not too bad (there was a shouting voice and an overwhelming pounding of drums and screeching of an electric guitar and the text was "he was the master of his slave"). It had the effect of helping Parker concentrate in this situation. Parker's son was holding out in his bedroom just above the office. Parker's son had brought his girlfriend home with him and she was up there with him.

It was Christmas vacation time. There has been too much stress during this visit and Parker had the feeling his son would probably be wondering why he had come home in the first place – nothing had changed – or so it seemed – Parker and his wife were still giving advice and trying to tell their son how to behave – as usual – or so it seemed. Michael had come over on the weekend after Christmas. Michael was the name of his son's friend. There was something about this kid that Parker did not like or trust. He was not sure if the phrase "did not like - or did not trust was correct. This guy was nothing but trouble and besides… what business did Parker's son have having friends over when he already had one guest – his girlfriend?

Just before Michael had arrived the whole family was sitting around the table – Michael bashing. Everyone had something negative to say about this boy. At one point it was too much for Parker. He could not think of anything good to say about Michael either but he did not like this mobbing scene at the table – which was also embarrassing because they were doing this in front of Jasmin, Parker's son's girlfriend. For Parker she was still too new to be showing the less noble sides of the family's behaviour. But he couldn't stop them.

Parker's son was out picking up Michael in Varel. All Parker could think was – I hope my boy gets back safely. Parker's son had just gotten his driver's licence and Parker was no way quite yet ready to give up his worry about his son's driving abilities. Thank God Parker's son and Michael came home shortly and Parker was relieved. There he was again... that Michael guy that everyone had been busy bashing. He was sitting at the table talking to all of them. He had a shining smile – that looked a little plastic and a curved nose like a little elf. Parker could not look him in the eyes… was it shame or shun – he couldn't discern his motives.

A bit later Parker's wife was having an intensive talk with Michael. Parker picked up bits of the conversation … it sounded as if Michael was telling Hannelore about the problems of his childhood. Parker trusted Hannelore to get people to open up. Hannelore had a way of showing her concern to people in need. And they came to her often for support. Parker was always glad when she was helping others and leaving him alone. Then there were two sides to this "helping" ability and the other side expressed itself in the ability to criticise and judge. And this was the side Parker knew most well and he was glad to have her attention focused elsewhere and not on him. But Parker had the feeling that the talk was good for Michael and since he knew Hannelore also had ambivalent feelings towards Michael he thought this talk may help relieve the tension that had aroused by Michael's visit. All seemed well.

Michael was going to sleep in the office and before going to bed Parker asked his son if Michael would needing the mattress that was kept under Parker's bed. Parker's son said no. This was not necessary because Michael would prefer to sleep on the floor on a thin gym matt. Parker let this go because he was actually glad not to have the mattress in the office in the morning when all woke up. After Parker had been in bed for some time the door to the bedroom flew open and in came Parker's daughter. She wanted the mattress! She felt it was impolite to make Michael sleep on the floor. And … there he was … this Parker… he got angry for the moment! Why was she getting involved? For Parker – the decision had been made and Parker knew it would have been better to get out the mattress but be it for laziness or because he had been glad that the office was not going to be messy… or for what reason… the issue had been decided … and now his daughter was overriding his "authority" Parker's reaction was automatic… like a knee jerk… he was mad… For Parker's wife his reaction was clearly out of line and she quickly used her critiquing ability in no uncertain terms… And the "stress" of Michael' visit was complete. Parker had tried to keep out of the stress … but there he was … by his reaction this the "mattress action" he was sucked in…   And to make things worse Michael watched the whole affair and how embarrassing to get the feeling that Parker was being angry and violent just like the stories Parker had heard about Michaels's parents. This was the reason in the first place that Michael was staying the night at Parker's place.

Nachdem sie vom Arzt nach Hause gekommen war

Nachdem sie vom Arzt nach Hause gekommen war, war sie sehr gereizt. Alles was er tat war falsch. Sie warf ihm vor nur sich um sich selbst zu kümmern. Er wusste was los war bei ihr. Wenn sie gereizt ist, ist er dran. Sie meckert rum, dass er entweder nichts für tut oder alles was er tut, auch wenn er nichts tut ist falsch. Er haute ins Arbeitszimmer ab aber sie kam kurze Zeit später und meckerte ihn aus dem Zimmer raus. Er musste mit um zu versuchen ihr Gemüt zu besänftigen. Sie aber kritisierte ihn lustig weiter, er fand das nicht schön, aber er ließ sich nicht provozieren. Er war Geduldig und noch dazu entschuldigte er sich bei ihr, dass er sich nicht genug um sie gekümmert hatte. Allmählich beruhigte sie sich und hat sich sogar entschuldigt für bei ihm.

Parker - Creative activity for the day

Parker did not belong in Germany. Or did he? He loved to write. Parker thought to himself; if I did not have anything to complain about then I would not have anything to write about. So maybe it was good to be in Germany where he had felt so much dissatisfaction:

06 Sept 2009

Dear Nancy,

Daria gave me a mini Laptop for my birthday. I am writing this letter to you with Microsoft Works that came with the Computer.

 I am lying in bed writing you this letter. It is cool because I have an USB Keyboard and can lie on my back and write this letter in a very comfortable position.

The lap top is sitting on the table next to my bed. I only need to look over at the Laptop every now and then to see that I am not typing bullshit.

Hannelore is sleeping in the guest room. She is maximally stressed out and needs her rest. Everything is bothering her, too much work and too little money. I am listening to Music given to me by Gesa. And the atmosphere is just nice...

I have wanted a mini Laptop for a long time now so I could be mobile and move round the house and write while being not too far from the rest of the crew. I want to be creative - but it takes more than "just wanting to" But for me this letter is my creative activity for the day -

I am working at Avarto services, in the Condor team. I have been in the call center for one year now. I have been in Germany for almost 26 years now. Time flies and life moves on…Cat Stevens sings "Oh very young... What will you leave us this time; -You're only dancing on the earth for a short while." And so is our youth come and gone -

If I cannot think of anything to write I can always quote my old letters I still have all the old ones I wrote on the computer way in 1993.

Thank you for the 2 packages I received from you. This week I got a lot of mail from the U.S.! Your package with the stuffed animal and T-shirt and the nursing book came this week and I got a letter from Marti yesterday and today a package came from Mom. I hope you got my present to you in the meantime. Getting mail and postage and writing letters is a big part of my life. I have been too busy to write very often in the past several months. By the way, what was the price of the book that you sent me? I don't expect you to just send me free books. And when you sent a book then use surface mail and book rate. It is a lot cheaper. I can wait the extra few weeks that it takes. The Medical Surgical Nursing book is very useful to me. I can already tell you now more accurately and better what the surgical recovery ward that I have been working in specializes in. For example, Most of our patients have disorders of digestion and elimination. Some of the disorders are colorectal cancer, ulcerative colitis, Cohn's disease and cholecystitis and then we have cases of minor head traumas and some cases of Cystitis. Several of our patients have Diabetes Mellitus; to go along with their other disorders. The greatest amount of my time on the ward is taken up with washing patients, checking their vital signs, passing out meals and bringing patients down to diagnostic tests or therapies.

By the time you get this letter my first tour of duty in the hospital will be over already. We are just finishing up 4 months work in a ward and now in April and May we are having another block of 8 weeks of theory. I will dedicate another letter to telling you about the various disorders that we have covered so far in our classroom instruction.

17 March 1994 © St. Patrick's Day.

You are probably working and there are probably special events and special prices being offered today. In Germany no one even knows or cares about it. I was listening to American Forces Radio out of Frankfurt this morning or I would not have even realized it. Today I took a day off from work. It snowed a little over night but it is mostly melted already. The sun is shining bright through the bedroom window right now. Hannelore and I have the front bedroom facing the street now. It has become a beautiful room since we renovated it. It has a beautiful wooden floor "parquet" and a six door built in closet and light pinewood panelling on the wall. The room is very bright now and when the sun shines through the window the light pinewood colour is dazzling. I cannot wait until you see it. It is 9:00 A.M. I just dropped Daria off at school. Hannelore and Carl have gone back to bed and are catching up on lost sleep. The sun is shining on Hannelore's sleeping face and the sight of her and Carl sleeping peacefully is priceless.

Outside the world looks wintry with the melting snow but the sun is shining very brightly and the birds are chirping in anticipation of spring. We have our first spring flowers in the garden. They are called Easter bells and look like mini green and forest floor is just starting to get green. On elder tree the first green leaves have sprouted. Spring comes earlier here than in Michigan. By the way, Carl, our baby is sleeping in our bed right now and he looks so sweet. There is nothing like a precious little baby. He smells so good and his skin is so soft. Today he smiled for the first time. He is growing fast and he has grown out of all his first baby clothes already. He has gained 2 pounds and grown almost 2 inches already. When I look at him I think I have never seen anything more beautiful in my life. I know that I thought the same thing about Daria too but I had forgotten the overwhelming impression of the feeling. Carl has gotten smart and is nursing well now and sleeping good. He likes to be held while he is falling asleep and sucks ambitiously on his pacifier spitting it out from time to time and crying until we stick it back in his mouth.

I am constantly listening to the Jimmy Buffet tapes you sent me. If you have any more feel free to send them. I listen to them on my 30 minute drive to work. One of my favourite songs is the song „It's My Job". And thanks for the newspaper!!! I enjoy reading a local newspaper from time to time. I hardly see anything American anymore.

By the way, could you send me copies of all your birth certificates of you, Jud and your kids?? I am still working slowly but surely on putting together historical documents of the family. I am going to write Arkansas and Missouri State vital statistics offices and try to get info on our great, great grandfather and grandmother of Mom's side. I think it is exciting to know that our great-great grandfather came from Germany when he was 3 years old. I do not know where he came from exactly yet.

Today I have a day of vacation. School was cancelled on Wednesday, our normal day for classroom instruction so I took 2 days vacation because there were so many people working on the ward that it would have been crowded so the head nurse offered that I could take some vacation if I wanted. I get 29 days of paid vacation a year.

Tomorrow I work from 7:00 AM to 3:00 PM. Then I work Saturday and Sunday from 1:00 PM to 9:00 PM and then Monday until Friday days. Then my tour on my first ward is finished. Then I have 2 months of school again.

Well that is all for now. I hope to write soon. Love Jim

Parker   in November 1975 and he is going crazy

Something just came up with Laura. All these days I've been saying that Laura was special to me. Well, I still like to think she is but I just don't understand this situation.

For example: I came over to talk to her. We exchanged a couple of comments and then there was silence between us. Then Laura moved away. It happened last night too. I wanted to talk to her but she said, "I am going to bed now." Then this happened several times on the same weekend retreat. It happened in the hallway and in Tim's room. I guess I will just stick by. "Laura, will you ever change?"

(I thought we were friends and we had something in common. But I met Laura at our 25th class anniversary and she told me her memory of me. It was of a boy who had attention deficit hyperactivity disorder (ADHD). I was flabbergasted and my feelings were hurt when she said this to me.) I have know her ever since the first grade and liked her a lot)

November 1975
What is Beauty?
What is Wisdom?

What is Greatness?

How can I be sure of truth?

What are my true virtues?

Why do I have these questions?

Could it be of growth?

Will they exist forever?

Will the misery of uncertainty chase me through all my life?

Follow your own values.

How do I know my values are truth?

When somebody reads this will they think that I am trying to impress them?

Then on day there came the end.

The perverse, the pure, the wicked, the wonderful,

The suffering, the serenity, the light,

The darkness, all of men's inventions,

His games, his laboring, his thoughts,

All were resolved.

His shame swept away.

Man's shortcomings replaced by the total essence of the presence of

The one being who allowed him to be,

To exist, to fail, to choose, to create, to destroy, to live and die,

And all was as it was supposed to be in the beginning and in the end.

I must stop here for I cannot comprehend!

November 1975

Could it be just my face? Or has it become more than that?

What is it?

Recently, I thought it was more but today Mr. Shaw was asking me why? (Why - about what I did not write here)

All I could think of was, "I am so worried about my face and my breath."

I just clam up, back away, and want to get out.

They say when you cannot handle your problems you retreat or escape by drugs, alcohol or smoking or going crazy. And - I forgot to mention - robbing, stealing, etcetera. Well I think I'll retreat or get confused. (go crazy).

Parker's Crazy Idea of Coming to Germany

He was no longer at Michigan State University. But Parker had a flashback. It was thirty years later. Parker was having a cold. He felt miserable. Just as he was feeling very down his daughter came bursting with energy through the door. She had always cheered him up. She was jabbering on about a feature she had heard on the radio on her way there, in the car. It was about some 84 year old famous author who lived in Paris and had just published a fourth volume of personal journal entries. She said Parker was an author. He thought about that. How could he be author? All he could tell the world was a story of failure and remorse. Sure, he had read about such things as anti-heroes. People had written books about men who achieved nothing. Why was he even here?! Germany – of all places! He was here because of Julie and the professor. It was painful, like trying to clean tar out of your hair. And then what had happened? It seemed to him that he had forgotten everything he ever knew, at this point. Of course he hadn't forgotten everything he knew, but it was all mixed into one big powerful mass of emotions, indistinguishable. It all came down like a wall in front of him.

When Parker walked down the street of the little village in Germany where he lived, he knew he loved that place but that feeling only went back to the start of his life here. Life here was like a story that had started somewhere but it didn't quite reach into his deep inner self because of some sort of alienation he sensed. He would rather be with Julie and the professor. That was what was important. He guessed that was what he was thinking and writing would be called *Stream of Consciousness*. The whole thing about thinking would had to have a structure of it were lead anywhere. The whole process of thinking was painful. And the structure of his life was like a vast ocean and he was riding upon the waves with no landmarks. At Michigan State the professor had inspired him but without the professor he had lost his direction. He had found the professor because of Julie. She had taken some courses in German and he followed her like a puppy dog. He had thought he would take a couple of courses with her get to know her better. But the professor had inspired him beyond that. The professor talked to him about famous Germans who had asked themselves questions such as: "What is beauty?" That was Goethe. Up until then he hadn't even known who Goethe was. Now he was up to act 4, scene 43 in Faust II. *"Ja, und?"* he thought about Julie and the professor. The professor was always talking about those things.

It was 1982. What had he seen in 1982? It was Michigan State University. It was Wells Hall, 7th floor. It was spring. It was the Wonderful Spring. The money for the trip had been procured and all lined up. More loans that he would end up paying back over twenty years. But that was no matter. He couldn't see ahead 20 years. He was young. His daily routine was good. Get out early and enjoy the fresh spring air. Then he did laps at the campus pool. He loved the feeling after coming out of the MSU pool after his laps of swimming. Class started at 9:30. He went by the Union building to have a coffee before. The fresh air felt cool in his wet hair. The birds were singing and the sun was just coming up. The coffee smell in his nose was like a rush as he entered the building. In his favorite corner his booth was open. He sat down quickly in the corner and opened up his favorite book. Faust II. He opened up the state news and ran across the headline: Learning foreign languages mean complete emersion. That was what he was doing. It helped him forget about Julie. Faust II wasn't very interesting at that point either. The class was being taught by a 70 year old German professor. Before the end of his first sentence you fell asleep. That's how boring it was. Goethe would remain a closed book for him. Professor Schild's class was more interesting on the other hand.

The questions being considered in the course were: What is beauty? What is wisdom? What is greatness? How can I be sure of truth? What are my true virtues?

Seven years ago *in Germany* he had been asking himself the same questions.

1997. He had been so boring that Parker couldn't remember the professor's name.

Julie.

This is written from sunny Sacramento on June 26th 1979. The question was Julie drove him to German but also to Sacramento. Could you talk pathetically like that? That was where he went to get over her. No way. It's 2012. . Julie had been a chance of honestly being loved and having someone to love. His soul mate for instance. That's what he had thought he had lost. Essentially it was his future that he had lost. How can someone be so dumb? What sort of a future would it have been? Wasn't it much nicer to have Laura and Jim? He was definitely over here but it had taken 25 years and one day he had woken up. It might have taken even longer. 30 years. But that had also been the day that he had lost his past - and his emotions.

Why do I have these questions? Could it be of growth? Will they exist forever? Will the misery of uncertainty chase me all my life?

Follow your own values.

How do I know if my values are truth?

"Then one day there came the end. The perverse, the pure, the wicked, the wonderful, the suffering, the serenity, the light, the darkness, all of man's inventions, his games and his thoughts were resolved and his shame swept away and replaced by love – the essence of the being who allowed him to be."

I must stop here because a man cannot comprehend more.

The ways of men can punish the spirit, causing the lonely man which he thought he was to reject his spirit. They leave his spirit weak like an old tree, perforated, robbed of its substance by insects and worms and it snaps and falls in the autumn storm.

For the end of the book:

In this life of mine the path I follow must be my path. It is not cleared by other. I endure and keep following my heart. Adrian, November 1975. What a strange prophecy he had made for himself back then, thought Parker to himself.

Parker was this the first story?

Professor Shaw and how Parker got out of high school.

Parker is being forced to write a story by his daughter. This is a terrible dilemma…so.

The belief that no project will ever be finished had long ago taken complete grip of his feelings. It was a matter of pride and a matter of - "what else was to be inherited if not a story – and - and still better - a story that sold and made money" Parker should have been making money all of his life anyway. He remembered his dad's failure at business. Parker's dad had failed in business before Parker was even able to write his name on a piece of paper. How could Parker have succeeded under circumstances like these? His dad's brother in law had a successful business. He did not go broke. And as a result they had the better houses, the better cars and his kids went to better schools. And to make the point – Uncle Billy always brought his old shoes and old pants and shirts and donated them to Parkers father.

Then later in Germany – Parker never made any money either. And Parker's sister and brother in law, Karin and Heinrich, were the "Uncle Billy's" of Parker's German life. They always had the better jobs , homes and cars and they were always bringing old TVs, Computers and furniture over to Parkers house – again because Parker and his wife had no money to buy these things for themselves. Parker had just about had enough of this nonsense. Everybody was making more money than him. Parker's wife was having a marriage contract drawn up to unsure that he did not get any of the goods that she had amassed since he had been living with her like used TVs and Computers. This was the absolute pits and he cursed the day he ever moved together with her.

Parker had cooked soup for lunch. His wife had suggested pancakes but that had not appcalcd to him this morning. His soup was too sharp and too salty and she only ate half a bowl. The strawberries he has lovingly bought were too hard and not sweet enough. And at the same time his daughter was there and she had been discussing her brother's drivers training – It was very expensive in Germany – Actually no one had the money to spear for this but it had to be achieved. Parker's son had applied for a job at the supermarket stocking shelves – but this would not start for 2 or 3 weeks and up until now not a penny had been earned by him toward his 2000 Euro expensive drivers training. Therefore Parker's wife was disappointed by lunch and immensely angry at being asked to pay for the drivers training before her son had even earned a cent. Parker felt like a dip shit because with his salary at the call center he could not pay for anything extra – he could contribute maybe 80 Euros per month. That was not nearly enough to pay for the drivers training.

And the whole day had been a drag because the weather was dreary and he would have to return to work tomorrow after being on sick leave. The whole idea of going back to work had left Parker with a feeling of trepidation. He really wished he would never have to go back again.

Parker's wife went to bed angry after lunch with no word of thanks. It always hurt Parkers feelings when she went to take a nap and did not invite him. The day before she had also not invited him to take a nap with her – Still he had gone up to their room to take a nap. Then very shortly he had been rudely awakened with the comment, "You're snoring! "This was because he had a cold and could not breathe through his nose. So - all in all - he was thinking how wonderful it was to be here and be married to his wife.

Über den Autor (2021) James Evers

James is an American expatriate. He studied „German Language and Literature"at Michigan State University from 1977 to 1983. He graduated den with a Bachelor of Arts B.A. later he studied for Master degree at the FernUni Hagen and received his Master of Arts „M.A Europäische Moderne: Geschichte und Literatur". James has lived and worked since 1983 in Niedersachsen in Germany. He has also been trained since 1997 as a Nurse in Germany and since 2008 as Book Merchant.

Weitere Titel erschienen von James Evers:

Die Rolle der Balkankonflikte vor dem Ausbruch des Ersten Weltkriegs.: Vom Scheitern der europäischen Krisenpolitik in Europa am Vorabend der Katastrophe.

Author - James Evers

Publisher: BoD – Books on Demand, 2021

ISBN 3753487260, 9783753487267

Length - 88 pages